"You're going to be stuck in Kings Corners longer than you'd like," Bud said with satisfaction.

"Not stuck," Teal answered sharply. "Detained."

"Teal, what is it about me that annoys you? My lack of manners? My personal hygiene? Maybe the big wart on the end of my nose or the way I carry most of my weight in my rear end? Come on, tell me what always bends you out of shape when I'm around?"

"There's nothing wrong with your rear end," Teal said without thinking. There was nothing wrong with him. It was just that she'd been warned so many times to stay away from boys like Bud, it was hard to let her defenses down.

His dimples deepened. "Well, it gives me hope that you noticed." As she walked toward the door, he said, "Want me to tell you what it is about me that annoys the heck out of you, Teal?"

Her hand froze on the doorknob as his voice challenged her from across the room. When she failed to respond, he volunteered the answer.

"It's the chemistry between us, sweetheart. That hot, sweet chemistry that caused us so many a sleepless night when we were teenagers. The nights when we lay in bed, thinking of each other—me wondering what it would be like to strip that cool veneer from you, strip everything from you, and you wondering what it would be like to be Bud Huntington's woman. It's still there, Teal," he mocked softly. "You feel it and I feel it, and twelve years has only made it hotter, sweeter, and more tantalizing. . . ."

WHAT ARE *LOVESWEPT* ROMANCES?

They are stories of true romance and touching emotion. We believe those two very important ingredients are constants in our highly sensual and very believable stories in the *LOVESWEPT* line. Our goal is to give you, the reader, stories of consistently high quality that may sometimes make you laugh, sometimes make you cry, but are always fresh and creative and contain many delightful surprises within their pages.

Most romance fans read an enormous number of books. Those they truly love, they keep. Others may be traded with friends and soon forgotten. We hope that each *LOVESWEPT* romance will be a treasure—a "keeper." We will always try to publish

LOVE STORIES YOU'LL NEVER FORGET
BY AUTHORS YOU'LL ALWAYS REMEMBER

The Editors

Lori Copeland
Melancholy Baby

BANTAM BOOKS
NEW YORK · TORONTO · LONDON · SYDNEY · AUCKLAND

MELANCHOLY BABY

A Bantam Book / November 1991

*If you would be interested in receiving protective vinyl
covers for your Loveswept books, please write to this address
for information:*

Loveswept
Bantam Books
P.O. Box 985
Hicksville, NY 11802

ISBN 0-553-44092-6

Published simultaneously in the United States and Canada

PRINTED IN THE UNITED STATES OF AMERICA

OPM   0 9 8 7 6 5 4 3 2 1

To Connie and Lucille Bennett. Connie and Lucille, I'm relieved that you didn't need to use the pipe wrench.

And to Linda Ladd, in Poplar Bluff, Missouri.

Author's Note

This story revolves around climatologist Iben Browning's prediction of a major earthquake along the New Madrid Fault, an area that runs from Marked Tree, Arkansas, across southern Missouri, to southern Illinois, and that produces hundreds of small earthquakes each year.

Through the summer and fall of 1990 the prediction caused quite a stir in parts of the Midwest. Dr. Browning had announced his belief that there was a fifty-fifty chance that a major quake would occur along one of several faults, New Madrid being one of them. His forecast warned that this quake would measure between 6.5 and 7.5 on the Richter scale and would occur between Saturday and Wednesday during the first week of December 1990.

Dr. Browning based his prediction on the pull of the moon's gravity on the earth's surface, but a panel of earthquake experts called his theory scientifically invalid.

However, that forecast alarmed the residents of

the area called the boot heel of Missouri. As December drew nearer, hysteria mounted. Dr. Browning's prediction put the New Madrid area in the national and international spotlight, attracting film crews from as far away as Tokyo.

Melancholy Baby

One

Egad. Not *Bud Huntington*.

Teal Anderson watched with resigned acceptance as the bus slowed to a halt to pick up the hitchhiker standing next to his motorcycle at the side of the road.

As the rider sprang aboard the bus, he shot the driver a friendly grin.

"Having trouble?" Orlan greeted.

"Yeah, I think I busted a sprocket."

The doors to the bus swished closed as Bud Huntington began to make his way down the narrow aisle.

With disgust Teal assessed the pair of grease-stained jeans and dirt-soiled T-shirt he was wearing. Same old Bud Huntington—without a doubt, still the most worthless resident of Thirty-One Corners.

Teal hurriedly picked up her purse and tote bag and set them in the empty seat beside her. Fixing her gaze straight ahead, she prayed that he would pass by and leave her alone.

For a brief moment she even allowed herself to hope that he wouldn't recognize her. After all, they hadn't seen each other in years. She had slimmed down twenty pounds since high school, and her hair wasn't shoulder length anymore, nor was it the nondescript brown she'd been forced to endure under her aunt Winnie's ultraconservative eye.

Pausing midway down the aisle, Bud casually inspected the seat beside the striking auburn-haired beauty.

Well, well, Bud thought. *Teal Anderson.* He was aware that there were other available seats on the bus—plenty of them, in fact—but none quite as inviting as the one next to Teal. An ornery smile began to form at the corners of his mouth.

Lifting his brows, he inquired pleasantly, "Would you mind? I get car sick if I sit in the back of the bus."

Nodding indifferently, Teal opened the paper she'd bought in Cape Girardeau, determined to ignore him as he went about storing her purse and bag under the seat.

Her nose wrinkled disdainfully at the odor of grease that came from his clothes as he slid in beside her.

"Thanks, I'd hate to puke up my socks."

She looked at him dryly, and he grinned back at her innocently.

Yes, same old crude, uncouth, unrefined Bud Huntington, she thought. *Some things never change.*

Snapping the paper open, she turned her attention to the morning horoscope, hoping he had enough sense to realize that she wasn't in the mood for conversation.

Apparently he didn't get her hint because he

began talking, saying things like "What have you been up to lately?" and "How nice it is to see you again."

Scorpio, she read, determined to discourage him. *This is not a time for speculation, especially in matters concerning the heart. Stay close to home in the P.M., and beware of Greeks bearing gifts.*

Frowning, she reread the prediction. *Beware of Greeks bearing gifts.*

The paper suddenly lowered, and Teal found herself staring into a pair of chocolate-brown eyes.

"I said, 'Nice day, isn't it?'"

Folding the paper, Teal resigned herself to the fact that he wasn't going to take the hint. The bus was still twenty miles from Thirty-One Corners, and it was pure folly to hope that she could complete the ride in peace.

"I think it looks like rain." Turning her head, she stared out the window at the passing scenery, not the least surprised to find that Bud had turned out to be an extremely handsome man. He had always been the best-looking boy in Widderman High—and the wildest.

As a young girl she had considered him to be overbearing and immature. But she had never admitted to anyone that in addition she had always found him incredibly sexy.

Deep down she had attributed her fascination with Bud to the fact that she had been raised in a no-nonsense, puritanical environment, by an aunt and uncle who were at least twenty years older than most of her friends' parents. Carl and Winnie had been good to take her in after her parents' deaths, but they had been very protective.

Teal had known that having anything to do with

a boy like Bud was out of the question. And if she had ever seriously entertained thoughts of going out with Bud Huntington—or any boy like him— she had carefully buried those thoughts away deep inside her.

A sound education and being prepared for the future—those were the important things in life, she had told herself, not some dark-eyed boy who wore his jeans too low on his hips, rode a motorcycle, winked at all the girls in the hallways, and wore his hair too long.

"I'm sorry about Carl and Winnie."

Bud's voice, gentle now, jolted Teal back to the present. Although he hadn't changed, his voice had. That deep, rich baritone would have caused a tingle of excitement in most women.

"Thank you." Tears swam to her eyes as she fumbled for her purse and a clean tissue.

He handed her the purse and waited until she'd regained her composure.

"The Andersons were good people," he said as the bus sped through the gathering twilight. "The town is going to miss them."

Nodding, Teal turned her face to the window again, not as a gesture of indifference this time, but because she couldn't speak past the tight knot suddenly crowding her throat.

"If there's anything I can do to help you . . ." His voice faded, mutely acknowledging that he knew there wasn't.

Teal studied the passing landscape, stemming back the tears. The boot heel of Missouri had been her home for the first eighteen years of her life. She could still recall her jubilance the night she'd graduated from high school. She couldn't wait to leave Thirty-One Corners. College and the opportunity to have her own business in a large city beckoned her. Somehow Carl and Winnie had understood, and Teal had gladly shaken the dust of Thirty-One Corners off her shoes and set out to make a new life for herself. Now, she was coming home for the last time, and she found the thought oddly disturbing.

The sun was an orange glow in the western sky as the bus pulled into the terminal. The passengers began to gather their belongings as Orlan called over his shoulder, "Just stay where you are, Teal. I'll run you by Winnie and Carl's on my way out of town."

Meeting his gaze in the large rearview mirror, Teal smiled back her appreciation.

Bud stood up and extended his hand. "May I say it's been a pleasure?"

Teal nodded coolly, having recovered from her earlier bout of melancholy. Gingerly accepting his grease-soiled hand, she shook it.

"By the way, I like what you've done to your hair."

Her pulse surged to her throat, and she was horrified to realize that he still had the power to make her react to his flattery. Bud Huntington had a line a mile long, and she knew it.

"Thank you," she returned stiffly.

"Yeah," he said as his gaze skimmed her short, curly bob. "Not bad—though I'm partial to blond."

Her eyes flashed with indignation. "Then you'd better run along and find one."

"Can't. I have a date with a sprocket." Giving her a solemn wink, he turned and made his way up the aisle.

Watching him exit, Teal wiped the greasy imprint of his hand off hers and wondered just how hopeless a man could get.

• • •

The headlights of the bus spotlighted the big red rooster on the mailbox Teal had painted in the fifth grade, the mailbox she'd so proudly given Carl and Winnie one Christmas.

As the bus came to a stop, Teal gathered her purse and tote bag. Orlan jumped out and opened the luggage bay and set her suitcase out on the grass beside the road.

"Thank you, Orlan." He had been driving the bus from Cape Girardeau to Thirty-One Corners for as long as Teal could remember.

Teal reached into her purse for a tip, but Orlan waved it aside. He touched the brim of his hat and smiled at her. "My pleasure, Teal. Sure sorry about Carl and Winnie. They were mighty fine folks."

"Thank you. They thought a lot of you, too, Orlan."

He nodded respectfully. "If there's anything I can do to help, you just holler."

"Thank you, I will."

He climbed back in the bus, and it roared off, leaving Teal standing in a cloud of dust and exhaust.

Slinging her bag over her shoulder, she picked up her suitcase and started walking down the rutted lane toward the old farmhouse that still needed a fresh coat of paint. For as long as she could remember, the old house had always looked as if it needed painting.

By the time she climbed the porch steps, her black leather pumps were pinching her feet, and she was sweating.

The temperature was in the nineties and the humidity was nearly a hundred percent. Miserable weather, even for Thirty-One Corners, Missouri.

She pressed the doorbell and waited for Ceil to answer. Carl's unmarried sister had lived on a three-acre plot down the road for over fifty years, but three years before, Ceil's health had begun to deteriorate, and Carl had insisted that she move in with Winnie and him.

Teal rang the bell again, wondering if Ceil had stepped out. When a few seconds had passed and no one had come to answer, she opened the screen and found a note pinned to the door.

Teal,

   Didn't know what time you'd get here. Gone to spend the night at Mildred Yarnell's. (I don't think Carl and Winnie would mind, do you?) Mildred fell and broke her leg, so I told her I'd watch her dog for her. I'll be home early in the morning, but if I miss you, I'll see you at the funeral home.

Love, Aunt Ceil.

P.S. The house is unlocked, so just go on in. If you're hungry, there's some chicken and a peach pie in the refrigerator. Eat all you want. The church ladies and neighbors have brought plenty.

Pushing the front door open, Teal made a mental note to talk to Ceil about being a little more security-minded. Thirty-One Corners wasn't a hotbed of crime, but leaving a note on the door announcing that the house was unlocked was tempting fate.

The sight of Carl and Winnie's dimly lit living room and outdated furniture brought a tug of heartache. As always, the blinds were pulled to prevent the rugs from fading.

Standing in the doorway, Teal closed her eyes and allowed the faint scent of honeysuckle to wash over her. For the briefest of moments, she was glad that some things never really did change.

She switched on a lamp and set her luggage on the floor, smiling as she spotted the old crocheted afghan folded neatly over the back of the sofa.

Her gaze traveled around the room with tender appreciation. Carl's brown leather recliner, worn smooth with age, still sat in the same corner opposite the new twenty-seven-inch television that Teal had purchased for them and had Ed Waters deliver the past Christmas Eve.

Moving slowly about the room, Teal touched the statuette on the mantel, the glass dish that always held peppermints, the fern that sat in front of the window. She stuck her finger into the dirt and shook her head. The soil was as dry as a bone. Ceil had never been known for having a green thumb.

As she walked into the kitchen Teal was heartened to see how neat everything was. Winnie had always taken pride in her home. The curtains at the windows were starched and ironed, and the faded linoleum on the floor shone with a coat of fresh wax.

In her old bedroom she sank down on the edge of the bed and lay back across the gingham spread.

She gazed at the familiar crack in the ceiling for a very long time until exhaustion finally overtook her.

Teal was up earlier than usual the next morning. The house seemed empty without Carl and Winnie's familiar chatter.

As she'd slowly awakened, she'd half expected to smell the aroma of bacon and coffee and to hear Winnie fussing at Carl for some minor infraction. But old house echoed only silence that morning.

The mantel clock was striking seven when Teal slid into the leather banquette in the kitchen nook.

Dipping a tea bag into her cup of hot water, she gazed out at the small patch of land that had provided a living for Carl and Winnie over the past several years. They didn't have many acres, but enough to raise the cantaloupes that they sold at a stand in front of the house. The money, though meager, had supplemented their retirement income.

When Teal had suggested the previous year that they might want to think about giving up farming, since they were both in their late seventies, Winnie had only laughed.

"Me and Carl retire! Never," Winnie had scoffed. "If we retire, we'll just sit down and get old."

So they had continued farming the twenty-five acres, and it looked to Teal as if they had been doing all right. The large cantaloupe patch beside the storage shed looked hearty to her.

Teal got to her knees and peered out at the melons and frowned. They looked as if they should have been picked yesterday. Another couple of days in this heat and they would be overripe.

Sinking back down, she mechanically stirred sugar into her tea. What was she going to do about all those cantaloupes? Surely, Ceil had thought to have them picked.

Ceil tends to be a bit forgetful, Teal reminded herself. That didn't mean Ceil was senile. She wasn't. The reason she forgot what she was told was because she never listened in the first place.

Teal glanced at the patch of cantaloupes again, and her heart sank. Living with Carl and Winnie all those years had made her too practical to allow the melons to lie on the ground, rotting, yet she had a nagging feeling it would be up to her to have them picked.

Mason. Hadn't Aunt Winnie mentioned in her last letter that Mason Letterman still worked for them? Rising, Teal decided that she would speak to Mason after the services that morning.

She rinsed her cup and set it in the drainer, then went to shower and dress. The funeral was at ten, but there were several matters that needed attending before the service began.

Harold Wilson, Carl's closest friend, had called to inform her of Winnie's massive stroke and Carl's fatal heart attack four hours later. "Carl just plain died of a broken heart," Harold had said matter-of-factly. "He couldn't bear the thought of living without Winnie."

Teal hadn't found that hard to imagine. Carl and Winnie might have fought over the muddy boots he kept by the kitchen door, but they wouldn't have parted with each other for a million dollars.

Once Teal had thought Carl and Winnie's devotion to each other was old-fashioned, but lately she'd begun to envy their relationship. There had been times in the past two years when she'd wished that she could leave the Washington rat race, maybe even find a man with whom she could share that same kind of relationship.

Shrugging off her melancholy, she headed upstairs to dress. By eight-thirty she was on her way into town driving Carl's old Buick Electra.

She had gone about a mile down the highway when a motorcycle appeared in the rearview mirror. Riding her bumper for a few minutes, the cyclist finally whipped out around her and gunned his way down the highway.

Apparently Bud's "sprocket" was fixed, she thought dryly as she watched the cycle disappear down the road.

I wonder if he's married, she mused, then dismissed the thought as something not worthy of consideration.

Driving into town, she became aware that it was growing and changing. But Kinderson Funeral Home was the same.

The big two-story house on the corner of Main and Pine still looked appropriately prim and proper. When she had been five years old, Teal had gotten it into her head that the funeral home was a kindergarten. She had nagged Winnie for weeks to enroll her there. Tired of hearing her whine, Carl had sat her down one day and told her what Kinderson really was, and she had finally piped down about wanting to go there.

She pulled into the parking lot and sat for a few moments, trying to prepare herself for the next few hours. The time she dreaded the most had arrived.

A pleasant Oliver Kinderson was standing at the doorway waiting to greet her as she came up the walk.

"Miss Teal," he said with his customary old-world charm, "I am so happy to see you, but so sorry about the circumstances."

"Thank you, Mr. Kinderson." Oliver had changed too. Gone was the tall, handsome, stately-looking man Teal remembered. Standing before her was an elderly gentleman, nearly bald, his once broad shoulders stooped with age. But his handshake was still warm and compassionate.

Oliver shook his head as he looked down at her. "Are you still looking for a good kindergarten?" he inquired.

Teal smiled, glad to see that the years had not been able to steal the mischievous sparkle from his eyes. "I'm always looking for a good kindergarten, Mr. Kinderson." Taking his arm, she walked with him down the hallway.

"I've arranged for you to have time alone with Winnie and Carl. Afterward, if you'll step into my office, there are papers that require your signature. If you would prefer to wait until after the service . . ."

"That won't be necessary. I won't be long."

"There's no hurry, my dear. I know you've barely had time to catch your breath."

"No, I suppose there's no hurry now."

Oliver guided her across the wine-colored carpet to the chapel. He paused just inside, his smile growing more tender. "If I can be of assistance in any way, please don't hesitate to call me."

Squeezing her hand, Oliver turned and left her to be by herself.

Two hours later Teal's hand ached from being shaken and squeezed. She'd been hugged so many times she was limp, but the outpouring of love had been overwhelmingly gratifying.

The residents of Thirty-One Corners had loved Carl and Winnie Anderson. Practically everyone in town had attended the double service. There were so many floral tributes that there wasn't room for all of them in the chapel. The crowd was so large that those who arrived late had to sit on folding chairs in the foyer.

Oliver Kinderson escorted Teal and Ceil to the long black car at the head of the funeral procession. Teal shook her head in wonder when she saw that both Main and Pine were lined with cars, their occupants waiting to pay their final respects.

"Oh, will you just look how everyone's turned out," Ceil twittered, dabbing the corners of her eyes with a lace handkerchief. "Everyone's just been so kind. Wouldn't Winnie and Carl be proud?"

Teal turned at the sound of a motorcycle pulling in behind the limousine.

Startled, she listened to the loud engine roar. Surely Bud Huntington wouldn't attend Carl and Winnie's funeral on a motorcycle, would he?

Ceil's voice was muffled as she blew her nose. "Oh, my, there's that sweet Bud. How nice of him to come."

"What is *he* doing here?" Teal snapped.

"Why, he was Carl and Winnie's physician."

"Carl and Winnie's *physician*?" Teal was dumbstruck, convinced that she'd heard wrong. *Bud Huntington, a doctor?*

Ceil nodded. "Didn't you know?"

"No, I didn't know. What happened to Dr. Grayson?"

"Oh, dear, you are behind. Dr. Grayson passed on."

"When?"

Ceil patted Teal's hand sympathetically. "Goodness, Teal, nigh on ten years ago."

"Aunt Winnie never mentioned it." Teal was beginning to realize that because she had stayed away there were a lot of things she didn't know about the final years of Carl's and Winnie's lives.

As Teal helped Ceil out of the car at the cemetery,

she noticed that Bud had parked a respectable distance from the grave sites.

Climbing off his machine, he removed his helmet and stood quietly throughout the brief service. The greasy jeans and T-shirt were missing this morning. He was dressed in a conservative three-piece business suit that even Teal found impossible to fault.

When the final prayer was offered and the last condolences said, Oliver began to escort Teal and Ceil back to the car.

From the corner of her eye Teal caught sight of Bud walking toward them. Pausing before the small group, Bud respectfully offered his condolences to Ceil before addressing Teal.

"Teal."

She nodded curtly.

Ninety percent of the town had sworn that Bud Huntington would be in prison by the time he was eighteen, but apparently he had defied Providence and made something of himself after all. Nobody had bothered to tell her that, either.

Teal saw the quick smile and the display of utterly charming dimples in Bud's cheeks as he read her thoughts. "Not many people call me Bud around here anymore."

"So I hear. *Doctor* Huntington, I understand?"

Teal could have sworn his expression told her to put that in your pipe and smoke it.

Speaking under his breath, Oliver supplied, "And Thirty-One Corners is extremely grateful to have him. He's one of our finest."

Color suffused Teal's cheeks. "You really are a doctor?" Teal realized that her astonishment was tactless, but *Bud* a *doctor*?

Bud's smile grew a little more distant. "Can you believe it?"

"I'm . . . I'm sorry. I was just caught by surprise," Teal stammered, realizing how rude she'd sounded.

"No need to apologize. I assume you weren't aware that I'd been taking care of Winnie and Carl for the past three years?"

"No. Winnie had never mentioned that you were. . . ."

He shrugged. "Maybe it just slipped her mind when the two of you happened to talk."

Was it just her guilt or was there a thinly veiled barb in that comment? The glint in his eyes challenged her to guess, but his words sounded strictly professional. "Winnie was a little absentminded these last few years."

Clearing her throat, Teal tried to compose herself. She found it hard to accept the thought of Bud Huntington as a competent, sympathetic doctor. "I understand there was nothing anyone could have done."

"No, it happened suddenly. Winnie had the stroke around nine. Carl refused to leave her side until she passed away at noon. He insisted on arranging her burial and selecting the flower arrangement for her casket. By four, the arrangements were complete, and he went home. When Fred Hyer stopped by the house at six to offer Carl his condolences, he found Carl sitting in his recliner, holding their wedding picture on his lap." Bud's gaze momentarily lost its coolness, and compassion replaced the earlier hint of arrogance. "He dozed off, and never woke up."

Teal nodded, fumbling for a tissue. "It's better this way. . . . They'd been married sixty years," she murmured. "Sixty years. I didn't even make it home for their last anniversary. . . ."

A white handkerchief was pressed into her hand when she failed to come up with a clean tissue. As she murmured her thanks, she realized that Bud was once again her benefactor.

"They were proud of your success. Winnie knew how busy your catering business keeps you," he said quietly.

His sentiment was appropriate, so why did it make her feel so guilty? Teal's lips firmed. He had no right to blame her for anything. She *had* kept in touch with Winnie and Carl. She just hadn't done it as often as she should.

"They said they understood why I couldn't get home as often as I would have liked."

"I'm sure they did. Where are you staying?"

"At the farm."

"Can you cook any better than you used to?" He smiled, warmth briefly touching his eyes.

The horrible family living class they had shared in junior high suddenly popped into Teal's mind. They had been "married" for one semester—the most miserable semester of her life. She had begged the teacher to pair her with someone else, but the rule had been that no one could change partners.

By the time she had suffered through several hours after school with Bud, preparing mock budgets, cooking meals, and planning a home and children, Teal had been ready to choke him. He'd refused to take any of it seriously. Instead, he'd delighted in watching her face turn the color of a tomato by making embarrassing suggestions about their "marriage ceremony," asking her about their "honeymoon" and how often she would consent to sharing "intimacies" with him.

"I cook well enough to suit myself," she returned crisply.

His gaze lazily assessed the lightweight cotton dress she was wearing. "Well, as I said on the bus, if you need anything, give me a call. Winnie had my office and home numbers written on a pad next to the phone."

"I won't need your help." Her response was out of her mouth before she knew it, and the directness of it embarrassed her.

"As I said, you have my number." He gave her a brief, two-fingered salute and walked back to his cycle. A moment later he straddled the big Harley, and it roared to life.

"You shouldn't have been so rude to the doctor!" Ceil scolded. "He was only trying to be nice."

Teal had forgotten that Ceil and Oliver Kinderson were nearby. They had heard the conversation. She felt color rise to her cheeks as the three proceeded toward the car.

"Aunt Ceil, he's the same old Bud Huntington," Teal muttered, wondering why she was so defensive with Bud. Why, after all these years, did she still feel so threatened by him? She was certainly old enough to make her own decisions about men, and though Bud had managed to escape landing in prison, he still wasn't her type.

"Bud might have been a ringer in his younger days, but he's a fine doctor now," Oliver said protectively.

"All the women in town love him," Ceil assured.

"I bet." In high school, he had been nicknamed The Greek because of his black hair, flashing dark eyes, and body of a Greek god. None of that had changed, so it wasn't difficult for her to believe that women still fell all over him. "And he loves all the women."

Teal got into the limousine, her eyes still following the dust trailing the motorcycle as it barreled down the road. As usual, Bud was riding like a bat out of hell.

Smiling encouragingly at Ceil, Teal leaned forward and patted the older woman's hand. The day had been long and trying, and both women were relieved that it was over. "Let's go home and get something cool to drink."

Ceil smiled gratefully. "That's sounds fine, dear. Just fine."

A moment later the long black car pulled onto the country road and headed back to town.

Two

"I like that particular shade of blue."

Teal glanced up the next morning to find Bud standing beside her grocery cart in the Piggly Wiggly.

She frowned. "What shade of blue?"

"Your blouse. That shade of blue is definitely your color." He picked up a carton of eggs and opened it to search for cracked ones. Satisfied that there were none, he placed the eggs in his cart.

"I'm thrilled you like it," Teal murmured, annoyed by the way her pulse quickened.

Bud selected a tub of butter and put it into his cart. "Actually green's my favorite color." His gaze lazily ran over her auburn hair. "Especially on redheads."

"Really?" Teal reached for a half gallon of milk. "I hate green. I don't have one green thing to my name."

"That's too bad. You should buy something green—maybe a sexy little green teddy."

"Why didn't you tell me you were Carl and Winnie's doctor?" she challenged coolly.

"On the bus?"

"On the bus."

"Somehow I got the impression you wouldn't be interested in my chosen profession." He selected a carton of orange juice. "By the way, I'd be sure the teddy was the right shade of green. Anything too flashy would lose its effect."

"I'll be extremely choosy." Teal placed two cartons of fruit yogurt in her cart.

At the end of the aisle they walked in opposite directions.

"What do you want to do with this, dear?" Ceil picked up a cracked porcelain vase and looked it over thoughtfully. "Looks to me like it just needs a little glue and it'll be good as new."

In spite of the heat, Ceil was wearing a dark cotton dress with a white collar trimmed in lace. She hadn't changed much in fifty years, Teal had decided, and she probably never would.

Teal glanced up to find Ceil studying the shorts and halter top she was wearing with a jaundiced eye. "Hot this morning, ain't it?"

"Sure is," Teal agreed.

"Still no call to go naked."

Teal ignored the observation and went on wrapping Winnie's Ballerina Cameo green depression glass pieces. She hoped Ceil wasn't spoiling for an argument. She couldn't bear the thought of wearing a dress in this heat, and she wasn't in any mood to hear one of Ceil's blistering sermons on the evils of today's decadent, gone-to-hell-in-a-handbasket society.

"Just pitch the vase, Aunt Ceil."

Ceil's eyes lifted to Teal in disbelief. "Throw it away?"

"Unless you'd like to have it." Teal fitted the last piece into a cardboard box.

Ceil studied the vase, shaking her head and muttering, "It's no wonder young people have such a hard time making ends meet nowadays. They waste more than they make."

Teal didn't answer. For some reason she couldn't get her mind off her encounter with Bud at the market earlier that morning. The man had a disturbing effect on her.

"Well," Ceil said, putting the vase in the trash, "I suppose it doesn't really matter. When the earthquake comes it'll probably get broken anyway."

Teal stacked the large cardboard box on top of another marked for storage. "What earthquake?"

"You know. *The* earthquake."

"Is there supposed to be an earthquake here in Thirty-One Corners?"

"You really haven't heard about it?" Ceil stared at her, visibly distressed that Teal was so uniformed. "Dear me, yes, we're supposed to have an earthquake. A *big* earthquake," she emphasized, in case Teal still didn't understand. "On the third of December."

Teal glanced up. "The *third* of December?"

"Yes."

"Who says?"

"Why, one of those climatologists. It's been in all the papers."

"Aunt Ceil, no one an predict an earthquake to the exact date."

"That scientist fella can. He said there's a fifty-fifty chance there'll be a big quake along the New Madrid Fault, and from what I hear, he knows what he's talking about. They say he predicted the San Francisco quake a week before it happened."

Teal reached for an empty box. "Honesty, Aunt Ceil, I don't think I'd put a lot of faith in that earthquake talk. Even with all the scientific equipment available today, no one has ever accurately predicted an earthquake," she reminded.

"Well, you can say what you want, but you won't find me taking any chances, and neither is the school system. They're having earthquake drills, and they're already planning to cancel school the first week of December."

Teal grinned. "You're not serious."

"I am, and don't you look at me like that. Everybody close to the fault line is taking this prediction seriously."

Teal had to admit that earthquakes were not unheard of in the area. According to Ceil, who began to lecture her, the area supposedly had over two hundred shocks a year that weren't felt, and fifteen quakes had hit the region in 1811–1812, all greater in intensity than the one that had shaken San Francisco in October of 1989. Three had been the most intense tremors ever recorded in North America.

"If this man's prediction comes true, half of St. Louis will be leveled," Ceil added.

"Half of St. Louis, Missouri?"

"That's what Edith Lawton says."

Teal smiled patiently as she began wrapping more of Winnie's crystal. "Exactly what is this scientist basing his prediction on?"

"Oh, I don't know. Something to do with the pull of the moon's gravity on the earth's surface, or something scientific like that. Anyway, some of the factories have decided to close for a while too."

"Jeez."

"I guess we'll just have to watch the animals," Ceil conceded. "When the big quake hit in December of 1811, they said the horses were skittish that day and even mean dogs came to their masters to be petted."

"Even the mean ones, huh?" Teal hid a grin as she tucked away another glass.

"That's what they say. There was this man who said that after that quake his horses and his dog wouldn't leave his side"

"Really."

Ceil blew dust off a picture, then wrapped it in newspaper. "They said that for days following the quake the birds not only lit on the man's horses, but they lit on him as well." She leaned over to bury pictures in the box she was packing. "The man said he saw wide, deep fissures in the ground and even smelled the sulfur coming out of the earth. Ain't that something?"

"That's something, all right."

"Must have stunk up the place to high heaven."

"It certainly would have ruined my day."

The sound of a car backfiring interrupted the conversation. Stepping to the window, Teal drew the curtain aside and saw Mason Letterman's truck pulling into the drive. "Oh, good, there's Mason. I was hoping he'd stop by this morning."

She dropped the curtain back into place and hurried to open the door.

"Why wouldn't he be here?" Ceil carefully settled another vase into the packing crate. "For the past ten years he's come to pick melons this time every morning during the harvest season."

"I know, but I was afraid that with all that's been

happening, Mason wouldn't show up this morning."

Swinging open the door, Teal watched as Mason, supporting his lower back with his hand, slowly climbed the porch steps.

"Morning, Mason."

"Mornin', little missy." When he reached the top, he leaned back on the railing to catch his breath. Teal wondered if the steps weren't getting too steep for him.

"I'd hoped to catch you after the services yesterday," Teal explained. "I really appreciate your coming by this morning."

Mason pulled a large red handkerchief out of the back pocket of his overalls and mopped his forehead. "Thought I best get on those melons early. Weatherman says it's gonna be a real scorcher today." Mason's face was as red as a hot pepper from the high humidity.

"It feels like it's going to get hot, all right. If you want, I can try to get you some help—"

"Wouldn't hear of it," Mason said bristling. "I don't need no help picking melons. Been doing it all my life."

"Well, sure, I just thought, since Carl wasn't here to—"

"No need to fret about me, little missy. You just go on about your business, and I'll get on with mine."

Teal watched as Mason turned and began making his way back down the stairs.

How old is he now? she thought. *Eighty? Ninety?* It seemed to take him a good five minutes to get back down on the ground and head toward the melon patch.

"You sure you don't want me to try to find someone to help you?" Teal called after him.

Mason waved his hand dismissively over his shoulder. "I know how to pick melons, little missy. You just go on with whatever you was a-doing."

Accepting his word for it, Teal went back into the house to continue packing Winnie and Carl's personal possessions.

As the morning wore on, Teal found herself going to the window frequently to keep an anxious eye on Mason. She breathed a sigh of relief each time she spotted his balding head bobbing up and down between the rows of ripened fruit.

Ceil emerged from the hall closet, balancing a stack of boxes containing Winnie's hats, just in time to see Teal walk to the window to check on Mason again. "Land sakes, get away from that window and stop frettin' so much," Ceil chided sharply. "Mason was pickin' melons before you were born."

"I know, but it's so hot and he seems so old. . . ."

"That's 'cause he is old, the old—"

"Aunt Ceil." Teal flashed a warning look. Ceil was a righteous woman who wouldn't allow an off-color word or joke to be said in her presence—unless, of course, she said it herself. And she could make more of the most outrageous remarks, voicing comments without reservation to people's faces.

Ceil calmly packed the hats away in an empty box. "Well, he *is*."

Teal had a hunch that Ceil's observations were nothing more than a case of sour grapes. She'd had her eye on Mason for years, but he had refused to be coerced to the alter by her endless batches of poppy seed bread.

To Teal's relief Ceil switched subjects. "I have a few days before I have to go to Mortwiler's, don't I?"

"Yes, it will take me the rest of the week to close the house," Teal conceded.

Ceil had made it clear at the breakfast table that morning that she wasn't crazy about the idea of joining all those other "pissants"—her word, not Teal's—at Mortwiler's Sunny Acres. Still, Ceil had little choice but to join the other nursing home residents, most of whom she had known since her childhood.

Teal had invited her to D.C., but Ceil had made it clear that she didn't want to leave Thirty-One Corners and be "hauled off" to Washington where she'd be "mugged and raped by some weirdo wearing a ring in his nose and his hair in a ponytail."

Teal had learned long ago not to argue. Once Ceil had her mind made up, trying to change it was an exercise in futility.

By mid-morning the mercury in the thermometer outside the kitchen window was inching toward ninety. When Teal went into the kitchen around eleven, she noticed that the tractor and trailer was still only halfway down the second row of melons. Mason apparently wasn't out to set any speed records in melon picking this morning.

How on earth could he stand the heat at his age? Teal was at the kitchen sink, mopping her neck with a damp washcloth. The barest hint of a breeze ruffled the curtain at the open window.

"Are you looking out that window again?" Ceil called from the bedroom.

"Just getting a drink, Aunt Ceil." Teal turned on the tap and let it run for a moment.

"You're just wasting time gawking out that window. If Mason Letterman can't take care of himself by now, he never will."

"I know, I know." Teal returned to the living room and discovered Ceil had abandoned her packing. She was standing in front of the mirror, putting on her hat, apparently preparing to leave.

"Are you going somewhere?"

"Yes, I have to do some shopping for my friend Pansy."

"Oh. Is Pansy ill?"

"Oh my, yes. She's a shut-in, you know. I promised her I would run down to Wal-Mart and get her some bottled water and some trash bags . . . though I'm probably out of luck on the trash bags." She checked her watch. "Yes, I'm out of luck on the trash bags. They're gone."

"Doesn't Wal-Mart carry a large supply of trash bags?"

"Oh my, yes, they carry a lot of them. But since everyone's worried about the earthquake, a body has to get there early in the morning to get them."

Teal picked up an empty box and set it on the couch as Ceil fussed with her hat and began pulling on her white gloves. "Now, dear, I need to show you where I've stored the water, the water purification tablets, the first aid kid, and the wrench to turn off the gas. It's very important that you turn off the gas immediately after the big jolt."

"But the quake isn't due until December," Teal reminded her.

"Still, you won't be catching an Anderson unprepared if it should come earlier," Ceil stated, motioning for Teal to follow her. "And it could, you know. It could."

Setting the box aside, Teal followed her into the bedroom.

Ceil reached under her bed and hauled out a thirty-gallon plastic trash bag and heaved the heavy bundle on the bed with a burst of enviable strength. When she opened it, Teal could see the bag had been packed with care.

The items appeared to be in a specific sequence: first aid supplies and various tools that might be needed to shut off utilities on top; followed by flashlights, a radio, and batteries; food and bottled water next; and bedding and spare clothing at the bottom.

"When the quake hits, the first thing you do is come get the wrench and turn the gas off," Ceil warned again. "Carl kept an extra one hanging on a nail by the well house in case the house was leveled and you couldn't get to my bedroom. Now, you're not to worry. I have enough canned food and water here to last us three, four days. Maybe more if we eat light."

Teal stared at the cans of potted meat and could almost assure Ceil she would be eating light, especially if she were confronted with an earthquake that could level St. Louis.

Ceil quickly bundled up her stash and slid it back beneath the bed. "I gotta go. Pansy will wonder what's happening to me. You won't be needing the car, will you, dear?"

"No, I hadn't planned on going anywhere."

"Well, then, I'll just be running along. I'll stop by Brownston's butcher shop and pick up some nice loin chops for dinner."

"That sounds great."

Minutes later, Teal was standing at the kitchen window, cringing as she watched Ceil back the big

Electra out of the garage. She wasn't at all sure she should allow Ceil to be driving. Winnie had mentioned in her last letter that Ceil now held the all-time record for speeding tickets given by the Thirty-One Corners police department.

As Ceil wheeled the car out onto the road and floored it, Teal shuddered. She turned away from the window wondering briefly if she should alert the town citizens that Ceil was loose on the streets that morning.

It was close to noon when Teal stepped through the back door carrying a large glass of lemonade for Mason. She didn't know if Mason would stop long enough to eat lunch, but she wanted to be sure that he at least didn't dehydrate.

"Mason," she called when she didn't spot the top of his head immediately. "Mason? I have a glass of lemonade for you!"

When Mason failed to answer, Teal set the lemonade on the fender of the tractor and started down the row. She paused, her eyes widening with horror. At the far end of the row, she saw Mason sprawled on the ground, a melon cradled in each hand.

"Mason!" Teal raced to him, knelt on the ground and searched for a pulse. *I knew it! I should have never permitted him to pick in this heat!*

She laid her hand on his forehead and found it damp and warm. His face was colorless, and he lay as still as death.

"Mason, can you hear me?"

Mason moaned, but made no attempt to answer her.

Thank God, he's alive. "Don't move. I'll call an ambulance."

Running back to the house, Teal phoned the local hospital for an ambulance. Thirty-One Corners owned one, and she prayed there wasn't another emergency at the moment.

She burst through the doorway again and ran back to Mason, carrying a damp cloth. She knelt beside him once more, bathed his face, and talked to him while she listened for the ambulance. When she heard a distant wail a few minutes later, she went weak with relief.

The EMT's were out of the cab the moment the vehicle came to a rolling stop.

"Over here!" Teal shouted.

Two young paramedics carrying emergency life-saving equipment ran down the row of melons, following the sound of her voice.

"I don't know what happened to him. . . . It may be a heart attack," Teal called as they approached.

She quickly stepped aside to allow the paramedics room to work. The young woman checked Mason's vital signs as her partner slipped an oxygen mask over Mason's face.

As they examined Mason, the young man voiced his findings into his two-way radio. A male voice responded over the airwaves, giving him precise instructions.

"Is it his heart?" Teal asked anxiously.

"Gramps, can you hear me?" The young woman leaned over Mason, calling, "Gramps?"

Teal took a closer look at the young lady and suddenly recognized that it was Mason's granddaughter, Janelle.

"Janelle?"

Janelle glanced up and smiled briefly. "Hi, Ms. Anderson."

"My goodness, I didn't recognize you. Why, you were just six or seven when I left. . . ."

"I'll be twenty next month," she answered as she went on about her work. She squeezed her grandfather's hand affectionately as the other paramedic started an IV. "Hold on, Gramps. We'll have you at the hospital in just a few minutes."

"Is it his heart?" Teal asked again.

"We won't know for certain until a doctor examines him." Janelle patted Teal's shoulder. "But don't worry. His heartbeat is strong."

The other paramedic went for the gurney, and minutes later Mason was loaded into the ambulance.

"You're welcome to ride with us," Janelle offered as the attendants prepared to leave.

"Thank you. I think I will." Teal scrambled into the back of the ambulance as the driver started the engine and turned on the red light and siren.

At the small hospital, Teal ran breathlessly behind Mason's gurney as it was wheeled into the emergency room. It was empty, except for a janitor who was guiding an electric buffer over the lobby floor.

A tall figure in a white coat with a stethoscope around his neck came striding through the emergency room's double door. Teal's pulse jumped when she saw that it was Bud.

Other than giving her a cursory glance, Bud didn't appear to notice her. He proceeded to examine Mason, his hands moving knowledgeably over the elderly man's body.

"Is it his heart?" Teal sidestepped as Bud tried to

move around her to the opposite side of the gurney. "It is his heart, isn't it?"

Two nurses joined Bud and worked as a team as Bud issued brief, concise orders. Teal waited anxiously for some signal that Mason would be all right.

"I told him that I would get him help if he wanted it," she murmured, practically wringing her hands. "I knew it was too hot for him to be out there alone, but he insisted he didn't want help."

Teal sidestepped again to allow Bud room on her side of the gurney, but they only ended up doing another awkward dance.

Taking her firmly by the shoulders, he moved her aside. "Stand over there, please."

"Do you think it's his heart?"

"Ms. Reynolds," Bud addressed a nurse, "I think Ms. Anderson might be more comfortable in the lounge." He reached for a clipboard and began to scribble notes.

Shooting him a pleading look, Teal began to protest. "Please, I only want to—"

But before she could finish, Ms. Reynolds had her by the arm and was firmly escorting her into the adjacent waiting room.

"It's his heart, isn't it?" she asked again as the nurse seated her.

"The doctor will be out to talk to you as soon as he's completed his examination. Would you like a cup of coffee?"

"No." Teal reached for a magazine, determined to keep her temper in check. She didn't appreciate being treated like a child, although she reluctantly admitted to herself that she had been in the way in the examining room.

After giving Teal a "suit-yourself" look, the nurse disappeared back into the emergency room.

Teal tossed the magazine aside, sprang from her chair, and began pacing in the waiting area. The smells and sounds of the hospital unnerved her, serving as a reminder of how she should have been with Winnie and Carl when they'd died.

Ten minutes later the double doors opened and Bud emerged, looking every bit the young genius Oliver Kinderson had touted him to be. Teal suddenly found herself thinking that he wouldn't be bad, even if he had decided to sell spark plugs in his dad's automotive store.

"How is Mason?" Teal asked anxiously as she hurried to meet him.

"He's awake now. It appears to be a heatstroke, but Mason has a history of high blood pressure and heart trouble, so I want to keep him here—at least overnight."

Teal wilted with relief. "Then he didn't have a heart attack?"

"At the moment I would say no. But that's not official yet."

Teal was finding it difficult to equate this cool, professional man with the wild and rebellious boy she'd known in high school. This man was so smooth, so self-assured . . . so attractive.

"Doctor." A nurse approached Bud.

Bud accepted a clipboard from the nurse, his dark eyes carefully scanning the form before he sighed it. Teal noticed the young woman's gaze lingering longer than necessary on Bud's handsome profile while she waited for him to finish.

That much hadn't changed. Women were still drawn to Bud Huntington.

As the nurse walked away Bud's gaze momentarily followed her shapely backside.

"Dr. Huntington, if I could have your attention just a moment longer." There was a slight edge to Teal's voice.

The frosty smile she was becoming accustomed to was back in place when Bud turned to face her. "Of course, Ms. Anderson. Is there something else?"

"Does Mason have anyone to care for him?" Teal wouldn't feel right about just leaving him at the hospital, sick and alone.

"His daughter has been notified, and his granddaughter, Janelle will look after him."

"I thought Mason's daughter was married to a California real estate broker."

"Thelma came home five years ago."

"Oh . . . divorce?"

"No, her husband was killed in an accident."

"Oh . . . I'm sorry." Teal wondered why she was suddenly finding it difficult to meet his eyes. She felt uncharacteristically awkward with him, almost as if they were on a handsome-single-man-meets-attractive-single-woman basis instead of just Bud Huntington and Teal Anderson.

"So was Thelma," Bud observed dryly while his thoughts ranged back to ancient memories.

She still has that air of superiority about her, only it's more subtle now, less tangible than it was twelve years ago. But it's still there when she looks at me. I hate that snooty, overconfident manner. It's hard to believe that at one time I had one hell of a crush on her, and she wasn't as good-looking then as she is now.

"Well, I suppose there's nothing I can do here," Teal conceded.

"No, Mason should sleep most of the day."

"Then I'll come back later this evening."

"Suit yourself." Bud turned and walked back into the emergency room.

"Suit yourself," Teal mimicked as she watched his incredibly broad shoulders disappear behind the double door.

An hour later Teal was still sitting on the bench in front of the hospital, wondering how she was going to get home. She'd tried to call the house, but Ceil hadn't answered.

She'd been debating for the past half hour whether to start walking and hope someone came along whom she knew or just to sit it out until Ceil got back from her earthquake-shopping-for-shut-ins to call her for a ride.

It was so hot she could hardly breathe, and the thoughts of walking was repugnant to her, but, Teal reminded herself, Ceil could be gone for hours. She frequently lost track of time, and there was no telling when she would decide to come home.

Teal glanced up as a motorcycle shot out of the clinic parking lot and streaked by with an ear-shattering blast. It was Bud again.

Deliberately looking the other way, she fanned herself with newspaper someone had left on the bench. She groaned inwardly as the motorcycle made a U-turn in the middle of the road and roared back in her direction.

Please let him have forgotten something at the hospital.

Bud brought the Harley to a halt in front of the bench and leaned back, balancing it with one booted foot on the ground. His white teeth flashed in his tanned face as he grinned arrogantly at her.

"Catching a few rays?"

Teal lifted her nose, determined to ignore him. Suddenly, she was aware of how hot, sweaty, and rumpled she must look. Her hair was falling down around her face, and she didn't have a speck of makeup on.

"Aw, come on, Teally," he mocked. "Get your nose out of the air." Now that he was out of the hospital, his cool professionalism fell away and the old Bud was back.

"Don't call me that."

"Sorry. *Ms. Anderson,* are you perchance without means of transportation home?"

"Don't worry about it, *Doctor* Huntington." Teal nearly choked on the professional title, but she supposed he'd earned it—unless he'd ordered his diploma from an ad in a magazine, which, considering his reputation, she wouldn't put past him.

As he lifted his heel to rest it on the handlebars, his face sobered. "The way I see it, you have two choices—either sit here the rest of the afternoon and then let me treat you for second-degree burns tomorrow or hitch a ride home with me, since I'm going right by your place anyway." His eyes openly challenged her as he reached for the extra helmet and extended it to her.

Ignoring the helmet, Teal said crossly, "Why would you be going 'right by my place'?"

"I'm making a house call."

"Right," she returned sarcastically.

"You don't seriously think I'd make a special trip just to haul you out there?"

Her eyes locked with his. "You don't seriously think I'd accept if that's the case?"

She hated to admit it, but he was right. She could sit here until Ceil got home, or walk and turn into one gigantic blood blister, or swallow her pride and be home in ten minutes, luxuriating in a tub of cool water. The cool tub won out over her pride hands down.

She reached for the helmet and took it from his hand.

"You know how to put that on?"

"No. It looks so complicated."

He was about to counter her sarcasm, but the warning in her eyes told him to let it pass.

Straddling the seat behind him, Teal took a deep breath, then locked her arms tightly around his waist. "Don't drive like a maniac."

He revved the motor a couple of times. "I wouldn't dream of it, especially with such precious cargo in my care."

The cycle was still burning rubber a block down the street.

Three

"Aunt Ceil!"

"Yes, dear?"

"Where did this green sundress come from?" Teal peeled back the tissue and lifted the dress out of the box. The color was stunning. A delicious shade of mint-green that looked good enough to eat.

"I don't know, dear. The box was on the porch this morning. I assumed you'd know who it was from."

With a sigh Teal packed the dress. Of course she knew who it was from. Bud Huntington.

Carrying the box to the closet, she experienced just a tinge of regret that she was going to put it with the Salvation Army things.

A smile curved the corners of her mouth.

The color really wasn't all that bad.

"I don't want hearts of palm. If I wanted hearts of palm, I would have ordered hearts of palm. I want plain old artichokes, Artie. And I don't care if you have to go to Jerusalem to get them!" Teal cradled the phone receiver between her neck and shoulder as she reached for the bottle of aspirin. "Put Phyllis on the phone, Artie."

A moment later Teal's secretary's voice came over the wire. "I'm sorry, Teal. It's a madhouse around here this morning. The pineapple for Senator Pierson's reception tonight hasn't arrived yet. What do you want me to do about it?"

"Do you have the slightest inkling where Senator Pierson's pineapples are?"

"Sitting on a dock somewhere in L.A. The dock-workers went on strike this morning. We still have those two cases of cherries in the cooler, Phyllis offered optimistically.

"Great." Teal tossed a third aspirin into her mouth and swallowed, wondering how Phil Pierson would feel about having cherry tarts at his luau instead of fresh pineapples.

"Mark called a few minutes ago. The butcher didn't send enough goose liver. Mark said if we expected him to have a hundred thirty-six dozen pâtés ready by four o'clock this afternoon, he's got to have twenty more pounds of goose liver in the next thirty minutes."

"Jeez, Phyllis. In *thirty* minutes?"

Phyllis must have consulted her watch because she replied, "Twenty-nine now. I'm telling you, things are crazy around here. Elinor's on the other line. She says she needs four dozen more of the emerald-green cloth napkins for the Wellington dinner-party tomorrow night."

"Then see that Elinor gets four dozen more."

"No can do. The supplier said he'd sent all he had," Phyllis countered.

"Tell Elinor to change the color scheme."

"Mrs. Wellington insists on emerald-green, and you know Mrs. Wellington."

Teal's head was beginning to pound. Yes, she knew Phoebe Wellington. If emerald-green napkins failed to appear on the buffet table, Teal's Tidbits would lose the Wellington account. At the moment that sounded tempting.

"We could try to slip forest-green past Phoebe," Phyllis offered.

"Perish the thought. Call the supplier back and tell him to check again. Surely the gods will smile on us and Walt will discover a box of emerald-green cloth napkins that the computer has overlooked."

"I'll see what I can do," Phyllis closed.

Putting the phone back in the cradle, Teal leaned against the counter and shut her eyes for a moment. She could remember a time when she thought that having her own business would mean freedom and financial security. Now she realized there was no such thing. Freedom had its price, and financial security existed only in the mind.

Teal stepped out the back door and paused long enough to enjoy the morning. It had been a long time since she'd paused long enough to enjoy a morning. With a searing jolt she realized that she had actually missed Thirty-One Corners. She had been working so hard to make her business earn a profit that she hadn't thought about mornings and fresh air in a very long time.

Taking a deep breath, she smelled the intoxicating scent of honeysuckle as she walked toward the melon patch. Unconsciously she began humming.

Ten minutes later she was carefully working her way down the row Mason had been picking when he had collapsed. If she met an unwelcome guest in the form of a snake, she was prepared to break and run.

Crouching between the rows, she gingerly pushed back the vines to lift each melon and check if it was ripe enough to pick. By eight-thirty, the service wagon attached to the tractor was full again.

By nine the tractor was sitting in front of the fruit stand. Ceil pitched in to help unload, wash, and stack the cantaloupes in bins.

Handing Ceil the last melon, Teal brushed her sweat-drenched hair out of her face and wished she had had the foresight to pull it back in a ponytail. "I'll be back to relieve you as soon as I shower and change."

"No hurry, dear. By the way, did I tell you that I moved the pipe wrench this morning?"

"No, you didn't say anything about it."

"Oh, I'm sure I did. You must not have been listening, dear."

"Why did you move the wrench again?" That wrench had been moved at least twice the night before. It was going to have jet lag if Ceil kept it up.

"Well, I was thinking. The bedroom really wouldn't be safe with all that furniture scooting around during the earthquake, so I thought, why don't I—just to be safe—move the wrench back into the kitchen. That was smart, don't you think, dear?"

"Whatever you think, Aunt Ceil."

"It's under the sink, right next to the jugs of bottled water I bought yesterday."

Teal settled the straw hat back on her head, wondering what Ceil would be like by the time December rolled around.

"Tonight I'm going to move all the glass jars to the basement, you know, the pickles and the ketchup and the steak sauce," Ceil added.

"Aunt Ceil, why would you want to go to all that trouble?" Teal climbed aboard the tractor, the horrifying image of at least *forty* jars of Winnie's pickles in the pantry flashing through her mind. She didn't want to lug all those pickles down to the basement! "I'm in the process of closing the house, and the earthquake isn't predicted to occur for months!"

"Well, you know what they say about earthquakes. They're unpredictable. If you'd just stop to think about it, the 'big one' could come just about anytime, and it would be such a waste to lose all those pickles Winnie worked so hard putting up last year. Now don't you agree?"

Teal nodded, trying to resign herself to the fact that she *was* going to spend her evening moving pickles and ketchup.

"Well, you'd better run along and get your clothes changed. I play bingo at eleven," Ceil reminded.

"No earthquake shopping today?"

"Oh my, no, I won't have time today. The earthquake-preparedness meeting is at two in the school gym. You can come along if you like. Everyone's welcome."

"Thanks, Aunt Ceil, but someone has to stay to work the fruit stand."

"Oh. Yes, I suppose you're right . . . but you don't mind if I leave, do you?"

"Not at all." Teal hurriedly started the tractor and drove away before Ceil could think of something else to move.

The fruit stand did a brisk business during the morning hours. Teal was surprised by the steady stream of cars pulling in and out of the graveled parking area. Dozens of men and women paused long enough in their daily routine to purchase the plump, succulent cantaloupes.

"Yes, sirree, I always did say that Carl grew the best melons in the whole county," Hugh Carlton told Teal as he paid for his purchase.

Teal smiled as she handed the ruddy-faced man his change. "Thank you, Hugh."

"It's a real shame you're closing the stand." Hugh wedged the bills into his billfold, then slid the wallet into the back pocket of his overalls. "Don't know where I'll buy my melons from now on."

"Oh, there are plenty of fruit stands in the area," Teal said.

"Yeah, there's plenty of fruit stands," Hugh agreed. "But there's no one around here who could hold a candle to Carl when it came to growing melons. Don't suppose you'd consider staying on and working the farm?"

"No, I'll be leaving at the end of the week."

"You know the business, don't you?"

"Not really. Uncle Carl grew cantaloupes for a hobby when I was growing up. I just helped him water the patch once in a while."

"Yeah, well, that's a shame." Hugh thoughtfully bit off a plug of tobacco, and Teal could see he was settling in for a long chat. "I hear you got you one of them fancy caterin' businesses up there in Washington, D.C. Guess Thirty-One Corners looks pretty plain after being up there with all them politicians."

Smiling, Teal busied herself with restocking the bins. Hugh was known to talk the pants right off a person if he wasn't discouraged.

"Guess you've met the president."

"No." Teal smothered the urge to laugh. "I haven't met him."

"Hear he's pretty good around the house. His wife, don't suppose you've met her neither?"

"I haven't had the pleasure."

"Well, she says that he insists on cleaning off the table, even when they send out for carry-out food."

"The president sends out for carry-out?"

"Yeah, that's hard to believe, but that's surely what they say."

"Well." Teal smiled at him warmly. "If that's what they say, then it must be true."

Hugh picked up his sack of melons and sent a stream of tobacco juice to the ground before he walked away.

At around one Teal was sitting behind the stand in a wooden folding chair fanning herself with her straw hat. Leaning over to pour herself a glass of ice water, she froze when she heard the sound of a motorcycle rocketing down the road.

Bud.

Springing to her feet, she pretended to be absorbed in examining the box of tomatoes Dan Latimer had dropped off earlier.

Bud pulled his cycle next to the stand and cut the engine.

"Good afternoon, Ms. Anderson." Even with her back turned to him, Teal could feel his dark-eyed gaze appraising her bare legs.

A shiver shot up her spine, and it annoyed her. She would not permit herself to be attracted to him—although she had to admit he was handsome. Doctor or not, he was still stuck in Thirty-One Corners, and she wasn't.

She turned and calmly poured herself another

glass of water from the thermal jug, drank it, then pitched the paper cup into the trash bucket.

"I said '*Good afternoon*, Ms. Anderson.'" He picked up a cantaloupe and balanced it in his hand.

Teal nodded courteously. "Dr. Huntington."

"You pick these yourself?"

"All by myself."

"There's a big old ugly bruise on this one." He handed the melon to her, then carefully selected another.

Teal pitched the bruised melon into the trash bucket, picked up her straw hat, and started fanning herself again. *You have to at least make an effort to be polite*, she ordered herself. *After all, he was Carl and Winnie's doctor.*

"What brings you out this way this morning?" she asked.

"Jim Dennison is ill. I was on my way to check on him when I remembered how much Jim enjoyed Carl's cantaloupes." Bud's gaze met hers, and she felt her cheeks coloring like a schoolgirl's.

"You hot?"

"No, are you?" That was such a dumb thing to say, she could have bitten her tongue off!

"By the way. Did the dress fit?"

"I don't know. I didn't try it on."

His brow lifted. "But you will?"

"I don't wear green," she reminded him.

Smiling, Bud casually sorted the bins for another melon. "Since you're closing the stand, I thought I'd better take a couple of melons to Jim before they're all gone."

"Since you're closing the stand"? That's it. Make me sound like the villain.

"I understand that Mason is doing well." The

inquiry was only a courtesy. Teal had called the hospital around seven that morning and had been told that Mason was resting comfortably.

"He is, if a crusty attitude is any evidence. He was determined to come out here this morning and pick melons for you. I thought I was going to have to tie him to the bed."

Teal smiled, picturing the sight of Mason and Bud going eyeball to eyeball. Mason should have known that Bud Huntington could be just as stubborn as he.

"Then it was heatstroke?" Teal still felt guilty about Mason's having been in the melon patch when he'd collapsed.

"The test results won't be back for a couple of days."

"But in your opinion it was only heatstroke."

Their eyes met, and Teal could see amusement flickering in his. "That's what I think, but, remember, you're talking to Bud Huntington."

Teal forced her smile to be pleasant. "I'm trying real hard to forget that."

Bud's grin remained as charming as ever as their gazes locked in a duel. Bud had the feeling that she had never liked him. And by the look in her eyes he wasn't scoring a whole lot of points with her right then.

Their gazes held as he tossed a melon from one hand to the other. "This one looks nice. Just plump enough to fit my hand, yet not too big. Just the way I like it."

Teal could feel the color creeping up her neck as his gaze strayed to the front of her T-shirt. He'd always had a way of making something personal out of nothing. She didn't know why she was letting him get to her that way. "I thought you were buying the melons for the Dennisons," she said coolly.

"I am." He made certain his fingers touched hers as he handed her the melons. "Sack these for me, will you, sweetheart?"

Giving him a dark look, she dropped the melons into a paper bag and handed it to him. "Anything else I can do for you, *honey*?"

His gaze traveled over her leisurely, pausing on her bare legs just a moment too long to be considered decent. "Nothing that comes immediately to mind."

Nodding, he turned and walked back to his cycle.

"Hey," Teal called. "When will Mason be out of the hospital?"

Bud continued walking. "In a couple of days, if his tests don't turn up anything new."

"Listen, I need to talk to him." Something had to be settled about the melons. The bank could take care of selling or leasing the farm, but it wouldn't harvest the melons for her. And if Mason couldn't harvest them for her, she was up that well-known creek without a paddle.

"Sorry, you and your melons are just going to have to get along without Mason," Bud called over his shoulder as he stored the fruit in the saddlebags.

"I need to ask him a couple of things, that's all," Teal insisted.

"You'd only aggravate him."

"*Aggravate* him? I would not!"

"I know you won't." Kicking the cycle into action, Bud revved the motor a couple times. "Mason can't have any visitors for the next few days."

He was off in a spray of dirt and gravel, riding down the highway without a backward glance.

Teal choked, irritably fanning away the cloud of dust that enveloped her as she glared after him. Darn his arrogant hide!

Stepping forward, she cupped her hands and shouted after him. "I only wanted to ask Mason what I should do with the melons!"

Realizing that he couldn't hear her, she let her hands drop to her sides in defeat. The motorcycle was already miles down the road.

She grabbed her straw hat and began fanning herself furiously, mumbling all the while under her breath. "Darn his patronizing hide. I'd like to tell him what I'd *love* to do with all those blasted cantaloupes!"

Four

Without Mason, Teal realized, she was in trouble. She couldn't return to Washington and leave the melons unattended. Carl had worked hard to produce a bumper crop that year, so she felt a responsibility to see that every last melon was properly harvested before the farm was turned over to new owners.

Thursday and Friday Teal mulled over the situation as she picked melons and worked the fruit stand in heat that could fry eggs on the sidewalk.

By Saturday she knew she had to have help. With the growing earthquake mania, Ceil had traipsed off early each morning, running one earthquake errand after another, leaving Teal to handle the picking and the fruit stand alone.

After breakfast that morning, Teal took the matter firmly in hand. As soon as the last dish was washed, she raced Ceil to the garage, determined to commandeer the car so she could make the drive to visit Mason.

"But, dear, Bowman's is running a sale on kerosene stoves!" Ceil wailed, struggling to dislodge Teal's grasp on the door handle.

"Aunt Ceil, I have to talk to Mason!" Teal wrestled to keep the upper hand, but Ceil was as strong as a bull moose.

"But if I don't get there when the doors open, we won't get a stove," Ceil argued.

"What in the world do you want with a kerosene stove in this kind of weather?"

"After the earthquake it will be easier to heat one room than the whole house," Ceil explained in a tone that said any imbecile should know that.

"Aunt Ceil! Read my lips. I'm in the process of closing the house. We are not going to be here in cold weather!"

"Well, you never know." Ceil reluctantly forfeited her grip on the door handle, but Teal could see that it was a hostile surrender. "You didn't think you'd be here this long, but now look. Without Mason to pick the melons, what are you going to do? Farm hands are hard to find, especially this time of year."

"I don't know what I'm going to do," Teal admitted. The problem had been the cause of several sleepless nights, but so far she didn't have a clue as to how she was going to manage it.

"I don't have to go to Mortwiler's until you leave, do I?"

"No, Aunt Ceil," Teal said patiently. "You don't have to go to Mortwiler's until I leave."

"Oh, good. Well, if you must take the car, bring it back the moment you're finished at the hospital. Meantime, I'll just go rearrange the furniture in your room."

"Hey, wait a minute!" Teal's hand froze on the door handle as she watched Ceil head toward the house at a dead run. "Rearrange the furniture in my room?"

"Yes, dear. Haven't you noticed that large print hanging over your bed? If that should fall on your head during the quake, you could be seriously injured." Ceil slowed long enough to look over her shoulder at Teal as if she couldn't believe Teal hadn't noticed the dangerous print. "I'll just move your bed to the other side of the room. It won't be any trouble at all. Really, it won't."

"Aunt Ceil . . ."

"You know, I've been thinking about moving that wrench again. The kitchen just doesn't seem the proper place for it—what do you think, dear?" Ceil looked up as Teal gunned the Buick out of the drive, ground it into first gear, then shot off down the road.

"Oh." Ceil shrugged, turning to go into the house. "She must not have heard me."

As Teal drove into town she noticed the area fruit stands were doing a brisk business with garden produce. She waved at Ned and Estelle Perryman, and they waved back as she motored past.

The city limits sign seemed farther out than she'd remembered. She smiled as she passed the population sign that read a whopping one thousand twelve—only the twelve had been crossed out and thirteen had been written in with a black marker. Jolene Ferguson had finally had her baby.

Tooling along on the open highway, Teal was surprised to see several new houses and several more under construction. Thirty-One Corners seemed to be enjoying a building boom.

The streets were filled with people. Lucille Gatsman spotted the Buick and waved as she was about to enter the Piggly Wiggly.

As Teal turned down Main she saw that Turner's Dry Cleaning was not Fenderman Laundromat. The hardware store had apparently changed hands, too, but Spartan Drugs was still there, with a sign in the window that announced that you could still get a double-dip ice-cream cone for a dime.

Teal was amazed to see how the town had grown. There were two video stores, a couple of quick-shop/gas stations, a flower shop, and two fairly nice looking dress shops that she couldn't recall having seen before.

In fact, there were a lot of things that she didn't recognize. When she'd been growing up, Main Street had been just that, the only two-lane street going through town. The buildings had been unattractive cement block and brick constructions. The town's one wealthy family, the Mettersons, had donated enough land for a city park. Mettersons Park was located at the end of the street, near the school, and in the summer the American Legion band played John Philip Sousa's marching songs there every Saturday night.

Teal cringed as she recalled how she'd suffered through those Saturday nights, huddled beneath a lilac bush, vowing to escape the banal little town the moment she was old enough to be on her own. Winnie had told her that she didn't know where she got all her "highfalutin ways," and Teal hadn't understood it either. She'd just known that she'd thought everything in Thirty-One Corners was as corny, nondescript, bland, and boring as the vanilla soufflé Lucille Gatsman brought to every church picnic.

But the town looked different that morning. Not that bad, actually. The newly erected wooden railings and porches on the stores gave Main Street a country look. Trailing begonias just getting ready to bloom spilled from hanging baskets on both sides of the street.

Mettersons Variety Store had an eye-catching emerald-green and white striped awning over the front door. Names of businesses had been carved into wooden plaques and stained a variety of colors.

Trees in large tub planters lined the street like toy soldiers. Benches stood conveniently along the way for the spit-and-whittle population to enjoy.

Old-timers sat and talked and young mothers with small children chatted in the shade. The word *charming* popped into Teal's mind. Charming and alive. Thirty-One Corners seemed to have received a surprising transfusion of life while she'd been away.

As she drove down Main Street Teal prayed that she would find a parking spot generous enough to accommodate the big Buick. She sighed with relief when she spotted a hole in the hospital parking lot big enough to berth the starship *Enterprise.*

In an attempt to avoid Bud, because she was bumping into him far too often lately, she scurried across the lobby, pausing briefly at the reception desk to ask for Mason's room number.

Mason's eyes were closed when she tapped lightly at his door a few minutes later. Stepping quietly into the room, she debated whether or not to disturb him.

She decided that he needed rest more than

company and was about to leave when Mason opened his eyes and looked over at her.

"Hello there, little missy."

"Mason, I'm sorry. I didn't mean to disturb you."

Scooting up against his pillows, Mason motioned for her to come closer. "You're not disturbing me. Just restin' my eyes. Sorry to leave you in the lurch with the melons and all. I'm gettin' out this morning, so I'll be back to work tomorrow."

"Oh?" Teal's spirits brightened. "This morning? That's wonderful!"

"Yeah, when the doc comes in, I'm telling him I'm leaving. I figure I've been here long enough."

"Oh." Her face fell. "Then Bud hasn't released you yet."

"I'm leaving today; don't matter what Doc says."

"Now, Mason." Teal pulled a chair closer to the bed and sat down. "You should think about this. You gave everyone a pretty good scare, you know."

"Sure, I know, but I'm all right—or at least as all right as anyone can be for a man my age. You gotta die of something, you know. Besides, I can't leave you with all those melons to pick. Carl would want me to see after you."

"Don't worry about me or the melons." Teal patted his wrinkled hand affectionately. "We're doing just fine."

"You're keeping the ripe ones picked every day?"

"Every morning at dawn."

"The Jamisons bringing their string beans over like they're supposed to?"

"Every day. Herb brought a big box by before I left."

"Good, good."

"Don't worry about the farm. You just concentrate on getting well." Teal patted his hand again.

She didn't know what she was going to do without him, but she didn't want him to know that. "I do need some advice, though—if you feel up to giving it."

"I feel up to anything," he said, bristling. "I'm not sick. What do you want to know?" Mason visibly perked up at the idea of someone needing his advice.

"Actually, I don't know anything about melons—except to know when they're ripe."

"Well, there's not a thing about melons that I don't know. What's bothering you?"

"Well, number one—how long does the season last?"

"Oh, you never know. We've had some pretty good rains, so the season might last three or four more weeks, give or take a day or two."

"A month?" *Jeez. Not another month of getting up before dawn, picking melons, working the fruit stand, and listening to Aunt Ceil fret about where the pipe wrench should be kept. I'll never make it.*

"A month," she said weakly as she patted Mason's hand again. "Well, that's not so bad."

"Good morning."

Teal glanced up to see Bud standing in the doorway. Her stomach had reacted with the same annoying little jump at the sound of his deep voice. With a wave of dismay, it occurred to her that after twelve years her adolescent response to him wasn't getting any better.

"Doc! It's about time you got here." Mason sat up, threw the sheet back, and pushed himself to the edge of his bed. "I'm leaving this morning. The nurse said you'd have to sign some papers before I can get out of here. So git to signing 'em so I can be on my way."

Bud stepped into the room and walked to the end of Mason's bed. He unhooked the chart, and his eyes scanned the information briefly. "You're leaving us, huh?" His gaze lifted to meet Teal's, then casually returned to the chart. "You're running a little temperature this morning, Mason. You hurt anywhere?"

"Nope, feel fit as a fiddle." Mason swung his feet over the side of the bed, making it plain he was anxious to leave. "Little missy here, she'll be taking me home."

Hooking the chart back to the bed, Bud smiled. "Well, if *little missy* doesn't mind stepping out into the hall a minute, I'd like to have a word with her."

"Sure thing, Doc. I'll get dressed while the two of you talk." Mason slid off the bed and shuffled toward the small closet.

Teal quickly averted her eyes from the sight of his bare backside flashing out of his open gown.

"Listen, I didn't encourage him to leave," she stated as she stepped out into the hallway with Bud.

"I didn't say you did." Taking her by the arm, Bud steered her into a nearby doctor's lounge. "Coffee?"

"No, I don't want any." Laying her purse on the table, Teal watched as he poured himself a cup and added a teaspoon of powdered creamer. "What did you want to speak to me about?"

"Mason. What did you say to him?"

"Nothing. We were just visiting."

"You know he's worried about leaving you alone with the melons."

"Mason knows that everything is fine." That

wasn't exactly true, but it was close enough. "I was careful to assure him he needn't worry about a thing concerning the farm."

Bud threw the red plastic stirrer at the wastecan and missed. He went over and tossed it in.

"Bud, how is Mason? Really. I didn't think his color looked good this morning."

Moving to the table, Bud motioned for her to sit down.

Teal shook her head and said quietly, "It's serious, isn't it?"

"Mason's tests came back this morning."

"And?"

"They aren't encouraging. He's ninety-three, you know."

"Ninety-three!" Teal's hand went to her heart. "Ninety-three! I had no idea."

"He doesn't look his age," Bud admitted.

"What are his test results?"

"His cholesterol is out of sight, and there's a small blockage in a main artery."

"A blockage? What does that mean? That's serious, isn't it?"

"It means that I need a few days to consider the options."

"You mean surgery?"

"I have to evaluate all avenues, Teal. Mason's age makes it imperative that he not leave the hospital until I decide how to handle this."

"What can I do to keep him here? He's adamant about leaving this morning."

"Thelma's on her way over now. I'll explain his test results. Once Mason understands what will happen if he doesn't follow doctor's orders, he'll agree to stay. He's an intelligent man."

Teal sank into the chair opposite Bud, feeling numb. "He's really not coming back."

"It could be serious."

"Then I've got to get someone else to run the farm until it's sold," she thought, unaware she'd spoken aloud.

As he studied Teal for a moment, Bud realized what was bothering her. "You're going to be stuck in Thirty-One Corners longer than you'd planned, aren't you?"

Teal lifted her gaze to meet his, wondering if his remark hid any deeper meaning. "Stuck? I wouldn't necessarily choose that particular word."

"All right. Bound. Duty has bound you here longer than you'd planned."

"I wouldn't say that either."

"Then what word would you choose, Ms. Anderson?"

"Detained."

He raised his cup, and his eyes met hers over the brim. "Frosts you fanny, doesn't it."

"No, *you* frost my fanny, Dr. Huntington."

"So tell me something I don't know." He set down his cup. "Tell me, Teal, exactly what is it about me that annoys you? My lack of manners? My personal hygiene? Maybe it's the big wart on the end of my nose or the way I carry most of my weight in my rear end." He smiled. "Come now, we're adults. What is it about me that bends you out of shape when I'm around?"

"There's nothing wrong with your rear end," Teal returned without thinking. There was nothing wrong with him, she finally admitted to herself. It was just that Winnie had warned her so many times to stay away from boys like Bud that it was hard to let her defenses down.

His dimples deepened. "Well, it gives me hope that you noticed."

Reaching for her purse, Teal stood up and walked to the doorway.

"Want me to tell you what it is about me that annoys the hell out of you, Teal?"

Her hand froze on the doorknob as his voice challenged her quietly from across the room. When she failed to respond, he readily volunteered the answer.

"It's the chemistry between us, sweetheart. That hot, sweet chemistry that caused us many a sleepless night when we were teenagers. The nights when we lay in bed, thinking of each other—me wondering what it would be like to strip that cool veneer from you, strip everything from you, and you wondering what it would be like to be Bud Huntington's woman. Ah, it's still there," he mocked softly. "You feel it, and I feel it, and twelve years has only made the feeling hotter, sweeter, and more tantalizing."

He lifted his cup and took a sip.

"I've never felt that way about you," Teal denied sharply, wondering how he knew. She had been so careful to avoid even looking in his direction when they were in high school. "You're just plain nuts." Her voice was barely a whisper as she felt a tingle trickle down her back. Her insides were warm and liquid as if he'd just thoroughly made love to her.

Bud negligently tossed the Styrofoam cup into the wastebasket, then stood up and stretched. "I know. I was only razzing you."

He slowly strolled toward the doorway. Just as he started past her, she reached out and grabbed the lapels of his coat. Her eyes pinned him vehemently. "Wait one minute. Exactly what was all that supposed to mean?"

"All what?"

"All that 'chemistry' insanity. Did it ever occur to you, Bud, that I might not be as cold and indifferent as you assume that I am?" Her tongue touched her upper lip smugly. "You have never seriously thought of me as a woman, have you?"

Their gazes were uncompromising as they stood in the doorway, facing each other.

"No, but I'm not ruling it out completely," he returned dryly.

"Well, do. And let's just be darn sure we know where we stand with each other. You don't push me, and I won't push you. While I'm here, it appears we will have to deal with each other. As you've pointed out, we *are* adults, so as long as I'm stuck in Thirty-One Corners, I would like to make this period of transition as pleasant and uncomplicated as possible. Do you agree?"

He lifted one brow curiously. "Stuck?"

"Detained!"

As he gazed at her, Teal wasn't sure what she saw in his eyes. Respect? Dislike? Indifference? Intolerance? With Bud it was impossible to tell. But why should she worry about it? Just because her heart danced like a jack-in-the-box whenever he looked at her didn't mean she could actually fall in love with a man who was destined to spend his life in Thirty-One Corners, Missouri, listening to John Philip Sousa concerts in Mettersons Park on Saturday evenings!

She wasn't a teenager with stars in her eyes anymore. She knew what it took to sustain a meaningful relationship, and Bud Huntington and Teal Anderson still had about as much in common as a wolf and a Yorkshire terrier. So if she were smart, she would avoid him and concentrate less on the color of his eyes and harder on getting the farm sold and getting herself back to Washington.

"Whatever you say," he conceded evenly. "We don't like each other. I'll try to remember that."

"Well . . . see that you do." She stepped aside, and he slipped past her and disappeared down the hall whistling.

Darn it. Why do I let him get to me like that? Why?

Teal dedicated her entire afternoon to trying to hire someone to take Mason's place, but all leads turned to dead ends. Anyone with potential had his own farm to run, and since this was prime harvest season, every hired hand was working someone else's fields from dawn until long after dark.

The only thing left to do was to run ads in the newspapers of the surrounding communities and hope that someone competent from nearby was looking for a job. By late that afternoon Teal had decided that she would accept anyone willing to work part-time. Anyone.

But placing ads and interviewing people meant a delay of a week or two she discovered, since the area newspapers came out only once a week on Wednesday evenings.

On the way back to the farm she stopped at a fast-food drive-through window to buy a hamburger. She felt a little foolish ordering a "Quake Burger Special," but she did it anyway.

The catering business will survive my absence

for another two weeks, she assured herself as she drove back to the farm. She'd spoken to Phyllis again the day before, and she'd been told that everything was running more smoothly. Phyllis had said that if there were any problems, she would call.

For the time being Teal knew that she had to be satisfied with that.

"Teal?"

Pushing aside her half-eaten hamburger later that evening, Teal called out, "In here, Aunt Ceil."

"Good lands, girl, why don't you turn on some lights?" Ceil walked through the living room, switching on lamps as she made her way toward the kitchen.

"It was light a few minutes ago." Teal shoved the cold hamburger back into its cardboard box. "Have you eaten yet?"

"Yes, Thelma Peterson talked me into going over to the diner with her. They have chicken loaf on Wednesday evening, you know." She gave Teal a disapproving glance as she entered the kitchen. "Without the car, I was stuck here all afternoon. Good thing Thelma offered to come and get me."

"I'm sorry, Aunt Ceil, but Mason isn't doing well, and I spent the whole afternoon trying to find someone to replace him."

Ceil sat down, her face sobering. "What's wrong with Mason?"

As Teal explained the results of Mason's tests, Ceil suddenly looked years older. "Guess I'd better go by and see the old geezer," she said absently.

"I think you should," Teal agreed.

"Guess I'll go first thing in the morning. I'm a little weary tonight."

"What did you and Thelma do all afternoon?"

"We had to drive clear to the Cape for flashlights. I had to have a couple more so I could finish Ruth's and Ethel's earthquake survival kits."

"Isn't the Cape a long way to drive for flashlights? Doesn't Wal-Mart carry them?"

Ceil leaned toward Teal, her face grim. "Yeah, but they were out of the ones with the big beams. Did you talk to Mason today?"

"Yes. Do you realize he's in his nineties?"

"Yeah, so what?"

Teal smiled. "So he shouldn't be working. He should be taking care of himself."

"Oh, pooh! Mason Letterman's a long way from being old, no matter what Doc says. I suppose Bud told you Mason shouldn't be working in the field."

"It may be a long time before Mason can work again." Teal sighed, toying with her cold drink. "And I can't return to Washington until I find someone to look after the melons."

"Yeah, you can't leave Carl and Winnie's place in just anyone's hands." Ceil checked her purse as if something might be missing inside. "Can't say I can be of any help to you there, but I don't have to go to Mortwiler's until you leave, do I?"

"Not until I leave."

"Good. By the way, I moved our earthquake survival kit. When Thelma came to pick me up, I showed her where I had it hidden under my bed. Well, Thelma said that under my bed wasn't very smart, so we looked around, and we decided to put it in the hall closet, the one beneath the stairs. If I'm not home when the tremors start, you run first thing and get it. And don't forget to turn off the gas—the wrench is under the sink in the bath-room."

"You moved the wrench again?"

"Where was it this morning?"

"Under the kitchen sink behind the two bottles of drinking water."

"Oh. Well, then, I must have moved it again. Me and Thelma anchored down all the furniture and mirrors too." Ceil yawned. "Gee, I'm bushed."

Teal smiled as she watched Ceil shuffle off to her bedroom. *Yes, I imagine you are.* If the earth-quake didn't get her, the preparation would.

Teal was awake before the alarm went off the next morning. She had slept fitfully during the night. She blamed it on the high humidity and lack of air-conditioning, but she reluctantly admit-ted to herself that it was because she couldn't get Bud off her mind. There was something upsetting about the way he kept appearing like a bad penny.

For the briefest of moments she had thought he was serious when he had said that there was a chemistry between them. Teal felt it, but she refused to acknowledge it to anyone but herself. The last thing she needed was Bud in her life to complicate it even more.

Around noon she looked up from the melon bins at the fruit stand to see Bud and two male friends go by in a pickup truck. A gleaming silver and black horse trailer was hitched behind the truck, and Teal could see two good-looking horses inside. Judging by the direction the pickup was traveling, the men were probably headed to Sikeston, a town about twenty miles away.

Ceil waved and called out as the truck roared by.

A black Stetson appeared out the window to return her wave.

"Guess the doctor's on his way to the rodeo," Ceil speculated.

"Rodeo?" Teal said, trying to keep her tone neutral. She didn't want to appear to give a hoot about what Bud did in his spare time.

Ceil nodded, handing Teal two heads of fresh lettuce. "The rodeo started yesterday. It'll run through next week. You ought to go."

"Oh, yes, the rodeo." The rodeo was perhaps *the* summer event of the year around there. Bud and his roughneck friends were probably heading there for a little excitement.

"Me and Thelma's going over tonight—soon as we visit Mason. We want to see Doc ride."

"Ride what?" Teal shooed flies away from the boxes of tomatoes. "I didn't know there was a motorcycle event."

Ceil chuckled. "The doc rides broncs, and he usually wins."

Teal looked up. "Bud rides broncos? *Bucking* broncos?"

Ceil nodded. "Ain't he a scream?"

"Yeah." Teal turned to watch the pickup disappear down the highway. "A real scream."

After a light dinner that evening, Teal wandered around the empty house, feeling bored.

Ceil and Thelma had left for Sikeston early, saying that before the rodeo they were going to eat at Lambert's, the house of the "throwed rolls," as they called it. They had invited Teal to come along, but since Teal wasn't fond of having food thrown to her, she declined. She had watched the two elderly women drive off in Thelma's Studebaker, wondering where they found their energy.

Teal was tired, but not tired enough to go to bed early. Besides, it was too hot to go to bed.

Retiring to the porch swing, she leafed through three magazines, but eventually she grew bored with reading.

The old swing creaked as she idly pushed it back and forth. She supposed that she could rent a video or take in a movie. An old James Bond was playing at the cinema, or she could just shop for a while, maybe buy a chocolate ice-cream cone at Spartan Drugs.

Leaving the swing, she went into the house, showered, and put on the mint-green sundress. She didn't have the heart to give it away, and she might as well wear it. Since her arrival in Thirty-One Corners she had lost her Washington pallor and acquired a golden tan from working outside all day, so the color was becoming to her. As she turned in front of the mirror she had to admit Bud had good taste.

Would he approve of the way she looked in the dress?

It didn't matter. She didn't plan on seeing Bud that night.

As she pulled out of the drive, for some completely unknown reason she couldn't begin to fathom, she turned the Buick in the direction of Sikeston.

Teal, you are not going to that rodeo, she told herself and meant it, but the big car continued to roll down the highway in the direction the pickup and horse trailer had traveled only a few hours earlier.

Leave Bud Huntington alone. You've made it

clear that you expect him to do the same, Teal kept telling herself. But before she realized it, she was puling into the rodeo grounds.

After checking her makeup in the rearview mirror, she got out of the Buick and locked it, a habit she'd learned in the city, though she didn't know why she bothered then. Carl had a sticker plastered across the back bumper that read "Make *my* day: Steal this car."

She bought a ticket and made her way through the crowd. The rodeo was already in full swing, the noise level deafening as the announcer's voice blared over the speaker system:

"Coming up is the bull ride, ladies and gentlemen. Tonight you're going to see some of the best rodeoing this side of the Mississippi."

Teal took a seat in the first row of the bottom bleachers. The view wasn't the best, but unless she wanted to climb up to the bird's roost, there wasn't much choice left in seats.

She told herself she was there only because there was nothing better to do. When she was growing up, Carl and Winnie had brought her to the rodeo every summer. Sitting there now, she could almost hear Carl's booming laughter as he took her hand and led her to the arena to participate in the calf scramble. The child who caught the calf with the hundred-dollar bill pinned to its tail got to keep the money, and Teal, who had been a half-pint then, hadn't let her size intimidate her.

Teal smiled as she remembered the year she'd won the prize. That darn calf had dragged her around the arena as though she were a limp rag doll, but she'd held on to it for dear life, simply more afraid to let go than brave enough to hang on.

After dragging the calf to the ground, she had emerged victorious, filthy, and ragged, but with a smile as big as Texas and a whopping one-hundred-dollar bill.

Those were the good old days, she thought. It hadn't seemed so at the time, but she knew it at that moment. No pressures, no business demands, no quarterly taxes, no traffic jams, no delayed flights, no rude customers or late-night subway rides with a can of Mace clutched in her hand. Her childhood had been spent in an easygoing manner she now found enviable.

Consulting her program, she listened as the announcer announced the bulls by name: Diablo, Midnight Fury, She-Devil, Eat Your Lunch. That last one sounded nice.

She looked up to find Bud leaning against the arena fence, the heel of his boot hooked on to the bottom rail. She had the unnerving feeling that he had been watching her for a while.

Smiling lamely, she lifted her hand and wagged three fingers at him.

He removed his hat and bowed ever so slightly to acknowledge her presence.

She was wearing the dress. The pulse in his throat beat harder as he looked at her. Her hair was swept up and pinned on top of her head tonight, leaving her neck bare. For some reason the word *vulnerable* entered his mind, and he wondered where it had come from. If Teal Anderson was anything, it wasn't vulnerable. She'd always been above it all—particularly above him. But damn if she hadn't been pretty, and that prettiness had turned to real beauty during the past twelve years.

Teal found herself scanning the program, fully

expecting to see Bud's name listed as one of the bull riders. Her eyes immediately went to Eat Your Lunch, and she breathed a sigh of relief when she saw that someone by the name of Tom Yokem had drawn that bull.

When she looked up the second time, she noticed that Bud had moved one fence closer to the bleacher where she was sitting. He was standing with two other men, deep in conversation.

Pretending rapt interest in the bull-riding event, Teal kept her eyes glued on the action, inwardly cringing as each rider was tossed to the ground like a broken toy.

Suddenly, one of the bulls turned and charged with its rider toward the fence on which Bud was leaning.

Teal shot to her feet, smothering a scream, as Bud and the other two cowboys scrambled away, barely avoiding the bull's horns as it rammed the boards.

Sinking back onto her bench, Teal realized that her knees were shaking.

When ten minutes had passed and she still couldn't locate Bud, she got worried. Coming slowly to her feet, she stood on her tiptoes to see if she could spot him. She knew that he had made it to safety, but she would have felt better if she could see him.

"Want me to hold you up?"

Teal whirled and then sagged with relief when she recognized Bud standing behind her, holding two hot dogs.

"You're crazy, you know that?" She sat down, embarrassed that he had caught her looking for him.

"Why can't you ever say anything nice to me?"

"Because you annoy me."

"I like to think that's unwarranted. If you could ever think of me as a man, a human being, and not as Bud Huntington, you might feel differently toward me," he said.

I haven't ruled that out completely," she mocked, paraphrasing his words to her in the hospital.

He handed her a hot dog. "I hope you like extra relish."

"I hate extra relish."

"It figures."

She grinned. "But I'll eat it anyway."

"Are you following me?"

"No!"

"Well, now, I'd find that easier to believe if I didn't bump into you everywhere I went." He took a seat next to her, trying to keep from spilling a soda. "I'm doing my best to avoid you," he reminded. "But it sure looks to me like you're deliberately hanging around my turf tonight."

Sighing, she took a bite of her hot dog. "That's what it looks like, huh?"

"Looks that way to me." His gaze traveled over her lightly. "I like the dress."

"Thank you. An old acquaintance sent it to me." In a soft voice, she added, "A very thoughtful old acquaintance who shouldn't have."

He grinned, extending his drink to her. "I only bought one soda. We'll have to share it."

"I'm not thirsty."

"That's what they all say."

They ate their hot dogs, both watching as one of the contestants managed to ride the full eight seconds.

"I didn't know you were interested in the rodeo."

Teal took the drink from his hand and sipped it.

"There are a lot of things you don't know about me."

He shrugged and grinned lazily.

Her gaze ran down his body, then she looked away abruptly. His jeans were too tight. They showed off his gender more than they should. And that red-and-green-checked shirt he was wearing open at the neck and the black Stetson tilted back on his head made him look arrogant—damned handsome, but impossibly arrogant. He didn't look like a doctor at all. More like a modern-day Jesse James.

"I think that thoughtful acquaintance of yours might have been too hasty in his selection. The dress is cut rather low," he said under his breath.

"And your jeans are too tight."

"Nothing wrong with my jeans."

"Nothing wrong with my dress." Teal self-consciously tugged the bodice up a little higher.

"Not if you're man hunting."

"Who says I'm not?"

When they finished the soda, he dug a candy bar out of his shirt pocket.

"A Mars bar?" Teal sighed. "I'm impressed. How'd you know I love Mars bars?"

"All women love Mars bars." He broke it in two and handed her half. "No kidding. What brought you here tonight?"

"A Buick Electra."

"And what else?"

She shrugged her slender shoulders. "No particular reason. I thought a rodeo sounded like fun."

"I figured you'd come hoping to see me break my neck."

She rolled her eyes. "Aunt Ceil told you."

His gaze softened. "So, you did come to see me."

She turned to him, her smile growing more mysterious. "I might have. What makes you want to ride a bucking bronco?"

"Because I like the challenge."

She studied him for a long moment. *Because he liked the challenge.* What a typical Bud Huntington response.

"Want another hot dog?"

"Yes, and get two drinks this time. Make mine a Dr. Pepper—a real one, not a diet one—and no relish on the hot dog. Just mustard, and not a lot, just a little."

"Jiminy, how do you keep your figure?"

"I'll worry about my figure. You just concentrate on getting the order right."

He tipped his hat politely. "I'll do my damndest."

Teal watched as he threaded his way back to the concession stand. She wasn't surprised to see that he seemed as comfortable in worn jeans and cowboy boots as he did in his hospital greens. He was certainly different from men in D.C. The men she knew were "suits"—the three-piece variety who carried bulging briefcases and tried to look important. That had never bothered her, until now.

When Bud returned, he motioned for her to follow him. He led her out of the stands to a picnic table under a spreading tree, away from the noisy arena.

"So, how have you spent your day?" he asked as he set down the tray of hot dogs and drinks.

"Picking melons and working the stand. How did Mason take the news about having to stay in the hospital?"

"How would you guess?"

Teal winced. "That bad, huh?"

"He wasn't happy about it, but he knows the alternative."

"Well, I can't say that I'm any happier than Mason about the whole situation. On top of being concerned about him, I spent all of yesterday afternoon trying to find someone to take his place—at least until the farm's sold—but I came up empty-handed. I've run an ad in the papers hoping someone qualified will apply, but it doesn't look promising."

"Have you listed the farm yet?"

"Yes. I'm hoping it will sell quickly."

"I wouldn't count on it. Not many farmers around here want anything under a hundred acres."

"I know," Teal admitted. "Uncle Carl's twenty-five, combined with Aunt Ceil's three acres, doesn't make a very tempting parcel."

"Oh, I don't know. The house is kind of nice."

"It needs a lot of fixing up."

"Maybe, but it has possibilities. I've always liked that big old wide front porch."

"Yeah." Teal sighed, leaning back to enjoy the starry night. "I used to spend hours swinging on that front porch on summer evenings."

Bud chuckled. "We used to sell raffle tickets on Friday afternoons in the boys' rest room. Whoever got the winning numbers that day got to ask out either you or Michelle Waters that night."

"Michelle Waters or me?"

"Yeah, it was unanimously agreed that you and Michelle had the best porches for serious necking."

Teal looked at him, shocked. "Are you serious?"

He grinned with lazy male assurance. "Sure. You didn't know?"

"No, I didn't know. You never asked me out."

He shrugged. "I never won the raffle—until tonight."

She looked at him and decided that she liked him. It was crazy, but she suddenly did. "So, what about you, Dr. Huntington? Other than being the town doctor, how do you spend your summer evenings these days?"

He shrugged again. "Riding bucking broncos."

"No former Mrs. Huntington lurking in the background?" she teased.

"No."

"Never involved in a serious relationship?"

"No."

"A meaningful relationship?"

He shook his head solemnly.

"An *interesting* date?"

Shaking his head once more, he tossed his empty can of soda into a nearby barrel. "They're calling the riders for the bareback event. That's me."

Teal gathered the empty hot dog wrappers and pitched them into the barrel as they walked past it. "Good luck. I know in the theater you're supposed to say 'break a leg.'"

"I don't think that's quite appropriate for a bareback rider," Bud conceded.

Teal chuckled. "Probably not."

They reached the fence and paused. They stood for a moment looking at each other, not quite sure what to say.

"Well, nice seeing you," he said.

"Yeah . . . be careful."

"You're staying for my event, aren't you?"

"Oh, sure, wouldn't miss it. How many times do

I have an opportunity to see Bud Huntington break his fool neck?"

They exchanged smiles and started to part ways when they both suddenly turned back and called to each other in unison.

They both laughed.

"You first," Bud offered.

"Oh, well, it's nothing important. I was just going to mention that I wasn't involved with anyone either."

"I know."

Their eyes met, and the noise from the arena seemed to fade. "You've dated several men on and off since you left Thirty-One Corners, but no one seriously. Two years ago you became involved with David York, an up-and-coming senator from Maine. The relationship appeared to be headed for the altar, but in February you broke it off, and no one but you and York seemed to know why."

Arching a brow, Teal stared back at him. "Anything else?"

"No—except I was a little relived when it didn't work out between you and York." He winked. "You had me a little worried."

He turned and started to walk off again, then suddenly spun around and strode back to where she was standing.

"Oh, what the hell. In for a penny, in for a pound."

He swept her into his arms and gathered her close. Her heart missed a beat as he lowered his mouth to hers. She held her breath as he gave her an instant to pull away if that was what she wanted. When she leaned against him instead, Bud took her mouth with a rush. Like a man who'd denied himself too long, he kissed her long and hard and deep.

She clung to the front of his shirt, drowning in the sensations that rippled through her. When he slowly released her long moments later, her head was swimming.

"Well . . . see you." His eyes locked with hers as he tugged the brim of his hat lower. With a hint of reluctance he strode off just as his name was called over the loudspeaker.

"Our first rider for the bareback bronc event is our own Doc Huntington. Doc's made quite a name for himself as a bronc rider around the state. Let's give him a big round of applause."

Teal lifted her hands and mechanically joined in the applause, her senses still zinging from his kiss.

Yeah, she thought, *see you around.*

Five

"Phyllis, I don't know when I'll be back," Teal confessed. She was down to praying for a miracle.

Her ad in the newspaper had been running for over a week, but no miracle had occurred yet. Only one man had responded, and he was already working two jobs to make ends meet.

"I just can't walk off and leave melons rotting in the fields," Teal said. "Just do the best you can."

As she hung up she experienced a sense of frustration that she hadn't felt in years. Phyllis was doing all she could, but Teal's clients expected her personal touch. Her reputation for perfection demanded that she personally supervise each step of every job, from the planning to the presentation of food, and that wasn't happening.

By the time the farm was sold, she'd be lucky to have a shred left of her clientele.

Picking up a stack of letters, Teal reached for her shoulder bag. "Aunt Ceil, I'm going to the post office. Anything you need from the market?"

Ceil appeared in the kitchen doorway, wiping

her hands on a worn apron. "You might get some of those little boxes of raisins. If Winnie had had any, I don't know where they went."

"Okay. Is that all?"

"You might see if they've got any more bottled water. They were out yesterday. You'd think those people at Piggly Wiggly would have enough sense to buy extra, what with everyone getting ready for the quake."

Teal gritted her teeth and kept quiet. It bothered her to see people who didn't have the money purchasing extra batteries, cases of bottled water, and flashlights anyway. Fear was replacing common sense. Being reasonably prepared was one thing, but panic buying was another. "I'll check on the water. Anything else?"

"Not that I can think of."

The Electra didn't have air-conditioning. By the time Teal drove into the Piggly Wiggly parking lot, her clothes were damp with perspiration.

As she walked out of the post office she spotted Bowman's Hardware and was sorely tempted to price a window air-conditioner for the house. She knew it was crazy. With any luck she was going to be there only a short while longer. Still, she couldn't help but drool at the sight of the large twenty-five thousand BTU unit sitting in Bowman's window as she walked by.

The rush of cool air as she entered the grocery store felt heavenly. Pushing the cart slowly up and down the aisles, she took her time making her selections. The bottled water aisle looked as empty as the Sahara Desert, but raisins were plentiful.

As she exited the store carrying two large sacks, she saw Bud's pickup coming down Main. Tooting his horn, he smiled and waved at her.

She smiled and tried to wave back, but the paper bags made it impossible. As she placed them in the trunk, she gave herself another lecture concerning Bud Huntington. She was bumping into him almost everyday. She wasn't sure if that was accidental or planned, and her uncertainty about which one of them might be orchestrating these meetings disturbed her greatly.

As she drove back to the farm her memory conjured up the sensations of the kiss he'd given her the day of the rodeo. That she didn't need. It was barely eleven, and she guessed the temperature was already in the nineties. Thoughts of that kiss heated her another five degrees.

She was midway home when she glanced at the dash, groaning when she saw the needle of the temperature gauge dipping into the red. Before she could decide whether to try to make it to the farm or turn back toward town, steam began billowing out from under the hood.

"Darn. Darn. Darn," she muttered, slapping her palms on the steering wheel.

She let the car roll to a stop on the shoulder of the road and got out. She looked up and down the deserted highway, trying to decide what to do. She didn't know anything about cars, so there was little recourse but to flag down a passing motorist for help.

Twenty minutes went by before she finally saw a car approaching. She stepped into the road and began waving, hoping the car wouldn't run over her. She sighed as the vehicle began to slow.

"My, my, my. Who have we here—and in trouble, again."

With a mixture of relief and dismay she recognized Bud behind the wheel.

She steeled herself for the flood of emotion that assailed her each time she saw him. This encounter had to be fate. She knew she didn't arrange it, and he couldn't have set it up.

She stepped up to his open window. "It suddenly overheated," she said.

"Need a ride? The car will be all right where it is until you can call a tow truck."

"Thanks."

Bud got out and helped her transfer the groceries into his pickup. When she slid into the passenger seat, she released a long sigh and blotted her perspiring face again with a sodden tissue. "I thought I'd melt standing out there in this heat."

The cab was cool, but Bud adjusted the vents so that the air would blow directly on her. She couldn't wait to get home, strip off her clothes, and stand in a cold shower.

Bud pressed the accelerator and glanced over at her with a smile. "You couldn't have been there very long. I saw you leave the market." The smell of his after-shave filled the cab, mingling pleasantly with the cool air.

"Long enough in this heat."

"It doesn't get hot in Washington?"

"Sure, but I have air-conditioning in Washington."

"Too bad. You look kind of cute all hot and sweaty like that."

Teal's body grew warmer as she turned her head to stare out the window.

The truck continued down the highway, and Teal noticed that they weren't going in the direction of the farm.

"Where are you going?"

"I'm on my way to Sikeston. Hope you don't mind."

"Bud." She looked at him, exasperated. "Why didn't you say you were going to Sikeston?"

"Now look. I asked if you needed a ride, and you said yes. You didn't ask me where I was going."

"I assumed you were going by the farm. Why didn't you tell me where you were going?"

"Because you wouldn't have agreed to ride with me."

"You're right. I have all those groceries I need to take home."

"What do you have that's perishable?"

"Well . . . nothing, I suppose, but Ceil will wonder what's happened to me."

He winked at her. "They have phones in Sikeston . . . and indoor plumbing and electric lights. We're real modern down here now."

It was late afternoon by the time Bud had finished his business, and Teal's stomach was pinched with hunger.

"How about some dinner? I'm buying," Bud offered.

"You bet you are," she teased. "And I'm going to eat everything in sight."

"Now I know why you're not married. No one can afford to feed you."

Taking her hand, he led her across the street.

"I think you'll like this place," he told her as he opened the door to the restaurant.

When Teal's eyes adjusted to the dark interior, her smile died. "Bud."

"Yeah?"

"Is this Lambert's?"

"Yeah. Have you eaten here before?"

"No . . . but I've heard about it. This is the place where they throw your food at you, isn't it?" she asked hesitantly.

Bud laughed. "Just the hot rolls. Come on." He took her hand and nudged her toward the hostess. "You're going to love it."

"Well, this is . . . unique," she agreed when they were seated a few minutes later.

A friendly waitress appeared with two enormous glasses of iced tea. "How you doin', Doc?"

"Fine, Beverly. How's it going with you?"

"Fine." Beverly smiled at Teal. "I know the Doc wants tea, so I brought you one too. But if you'd prefer something else?"

"Tea is fine." A gallon was a bit much, but Teal silently conceded that the extreme heat probably accounted for the generous amount.

The tea tasted wonderful. And so must the food, she decided as she watched diners nod to the waitresses moving from table to table, ladling second helpings of fried potatoes, fried okra, macaroni and tomatoes, and white beans onto plates that were already overflowing.

"Do you come here often?" Teal asked as the waitress walked away with their orders.

"As often as I get down this way."

A teenage boy was pushing a cart among the tables. When a diner stood up and motioned to him, the fellow tossed him a dinner roll the size of a grapefruit.

As it turned out, the rolls were the best Teal had ever eaten. The hot bread, fresh from the oven and served with butter and sorghum, literally melted in her mouth.

"What are the chances of me getting this recipe?" Teal asked as she reached for her second roll. Her clients would die for this treat.

"You'd have to move back here and marry me." Bud stood and motioned to the young man for two more rolls.

Teal buttered her roll, quietly considering the tempting suggestion.

The young man, apparently well-acquainted with the doctor, grinned wickedly and drew back to throw the roll harder than necessary.

Just for meanness, Bud, ducked.

The roll grazed Teal, sweeping her hair as it shot past her and hit the wall.

Bud froze. He thought it was funny, but he wasn't sure how she would take being hit with a roll.

With a straight face Teal leaned over and picked the roll up from the floor.

"Hey . . . sorry about that," Bud apologized.

"I should hope so." Breaking into an impish grin, she threw the roll at him.

Caught by surprise, he ducked and the roll whizzed by him and struck a woman in the next booth in the back of the head. The woman whirled around and shot the young man in charge of the rolls a vicious look.

Bud dropped back onto the chair as Teal glanced guiltily at her plate. A moment later her gaze met Bud's, and their eyes glinted with mischief.

"Did I embarrass you, Anderson?" he asked in a whisper.

"I could just die, Dr. Huntington," she replied, smothering a giggle. "Simply die."

Later, feeling stuffed and sleepy, Teal sat beside Bud in the truck and watched the scenery pass beneath a bright moon as they headed back to Thirty-One Corners. In spite of everything—the overheated car, the "throwed rolls," and another aborted attempt to steer clear of Bud—the afternoon had been fun.

She'd enjoyed his company. He was an intelligent, quick-witted conversationalist. Unlike how he'd been as a boy, he seemed unaware of his charisma. During dinner she'd found his sharp, self-deprecating humor outrageously charming. He was completely disarming, and she imagined that his bedside manner—in or out of bed—was just as devastating.

It wasn't hard to see why everyone in Mississippi County loved and respected him. Bad boy made good—or had he ever been that bad? Teal couldn't recall a single instance when Carl or Winnie had actually said anything unfavorable about Bud, with the exception of "He was just an energetic young un who'd been given more than his share of wild oats to sow."

As the pickup sped through the night Teal felt a bond growing between them, one she could never have envisioned before. Right then, it wouldn't be hard for her to imagine being Bud Huntington's girl. He seemed like a man she could confide in.

"What do you think about this earthquake thing?" she murmured sleepily.

"Worried?" He put his arm around her as she scooted closer to rest her head on his shoulder.

"No, but Aunt Ceil is. She's making all these elaborate preparations. She's moved her survival kit so many times that the trash bag containing it is getting frayed. Since I've been home, she's driven to Cape Girardeau three times to do earthquake shopping for her friends. Is she being utterly ridiculous, or am I just not seeing the possibility clearly?"

Bud smiled. "Iben Browning's prediction has a lot of people worried."

"Has he really set a date for the quake?"

"No, he's merely pointed out that around the third of December conditions are right for an earthquake to occur along several fault lines. New Madrid happens to be one of them."

"That's scary."

"No, the scary thing is the way the whole thing is getting out of hand. People living along the fault should be prepared, but they don't need to spend every dime they have on supplies while they live in mortal terror of December third. Browning has said there's a fifty-fifty chance that the quake will occur. Now, think about it. That means there's a fifty percent chance it won't happen, but people invariably choose to think the worse."

"I know. Ceil said that Thelma and two friends plan to leave town that weekend. They're making big plans to drive to Springfield, Missouri, to go Christmas shopping."

"There are a lot of people planning to leave the area that weekend. Haven't you seen the signs. 'Earthquake Escape Weekends'?"

"Yeah, and the 'Shake, Rattle, and Roll' parties some of the bars are planning."

"They say that every hotel within a fifty-mile radius of here is booked to the max that weekend by curiosity seekers and the media."

"That's almost ghoulish."

"It's news," Bud conceded.

"Well, I won't be here, but now I'm concerned about Ceil."

"Isn't she moving to Mortwilers'?"

"Yes, as soon as I close the house."

He was silent for a moment, then he said quietly, "Have you ever given any thought to moving back here?"

"No . . . there's nothing here for me anymore." Her finger toyed with the snap on his Western shirt. She was tempted to open it and touch the mat of dark hair she knew lay beneath. Suddenly aware of the direction of her thoughts, she let her hand drop away.

He casually reached for her hand and put it on the snap again. "What's so attractive about Washington, D.C.?"

The question caught her off guard. She struggled to control her suddenly shallow breathing, afraid he would notice, as her mind struggled to come up with a coherent answer. What *was* so attractive about D.C.? It was a big, crowded, noisy city. "Well, for one thing, my business is there. My friends are there. I'm used to it."

"Are you happy living there?"

"Most of the time. The city has everything I always thought I wanted. It's a lot different from Thirty-One Corners."

"Different how?"

"I don't know. . . . Just different."

"Such as?"

"You mean specifically? I don't know, Bud. It's large and exciting and interesting. There's the Smithsonian and the Washington Monument and the Pentagon and the White House. Have you ever been to the Smithsonian?"

"No."

"Did you know that they have the Fonz's leather

Passion awaits you...
Step into the magical world of

Loveswept

E N J O Y . . .

6 ROMANCES RISK FREE!

P L U S

FREE GIFT

Enjoy Kay Hooper's *"Larger Than Life"*! Not for sale anywhere, this exclusive novel is yours to keep—FREE— no matter what!

tach and affix this stamp to the reply card and mail at once!

S E E   D E T A I L S   I N S I D E . . .

A Magical World of Enchantment Awaits You When You're Loveswept!

Your heart will be swept away with Loveswept Romances when you meet exciting heroes you'll fall in love with...beautiful heroines you'll identify with. Share the laughter, tears and the passion of unforgettable couples as love works its magic spell. These romances will lift you into the exciting world of love, charm and enchantment!

You'll enjoy award-winning authors such as Iris Johansen, Sandra Brown, Kay Hooper and others who top the best-seller lists. Each offers a kaleidoscope of adventure and passion that will enthrall, excite and exhilarate you with the magic of being Loveswept.

* ♥ *We'd like to send you 6 new novels to enjoy—<u>risk free</u>!*
* ♥ *There's no obligation to buy.*
* ♥ *6 exciting romances—plus your <u>free gift</u>—brought right to your door!*
* ♥ *Convenient money-saving, time-saving home delivery!*

Join the Loveswept at-home reader service and we'll send you 6 new romances about once a month—<u>before they appear in the bookstore</u>! You always get 15 days to preview them before you decide. Keep only those you want. Each book is yours for only $2.25*. That's a total savings of $3.00 off the retail price for each 6 book shipment.

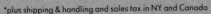

ENJOY . . .

♥ 6 Romance Novels–Risk Free! ♥ Exclusive Novel Free!
♥ Money Saving Home Delivery!

FREE BOOK OFFER
RUSH!

BUSINESS REPLY MAIL
FIRST CLASS MAIL   PERMIT NO. 2456   HICKSVILLE, NY

POSTAGE WILL BE PAID BY ADDRESSEE

Loveswept

BANTAM BOOKS
P.O. BOX 985
HICKSVILLE, NY 11802-9827

NO POSTAGE
NECESSARY
IF MAILED
IN THE
UNITED STATES

jacket, Hawkeye's gin mill from *M*A*S*H**, and Archie Bunker's armchair?"

"No, I didn't."

"And the cherry blossoms are lovely in the spring. You need to visit this spring, and I'll show you the sights. It's a wonderful city most of the time."

"And crime is bad all the time."

"Any large city has crime."

"Thirty-One Corners doesn't have much." He grinned. "Now that I'm grown up."

"I know it's hard to understand my position. When you went off to college and medical school, didn't you love experiencing a whole new world? Thirty-One Corners is . . . limited."

"Not particularly. At first being away was okay, but then I began missing the people, missing the serenity. I missed the sound of silence the most. I'll be honest with you, Teal, I don't like living in a rat race. No matter where I go, Thirty-One Corners always looks good to me and I can't want to get back home. I like walking down the street and having people call me by name, and I like the way people stop and talk a minute. Even the times when I have to refer people to a facility in another town for specialized equipment that we don't have, I still feel I've played an important part in their lives. It's a great feeling to be needed, and I never had that feeling when I lived away from Thirty-One Corners. I felt I was just one insignificant speck in the universe."

Good to be needed. Teal had never thought of it that way. Yes, she supposed it would be nice to know that there was only one you, and no one could quite take your place. "I can understand that. My business needs me."

"I'm sure it does," he conceded.

"You know how good it is to have your own business," she reminded, "to be at the helm of your own destiny? Unlike you, I couldn't have had my own business if I'd stayed in Thirty-One Corners. Actually, our lives aren't that much different when you stop to think about it. We both have good, solid careers—not bad for a couple of kids from Thirty-One Corners." She was aware that there was a touch of defensiveness in her voice and she didn't mean it to be there, but for some reason it was important to her that he understand.

"Yes, I left Thirty-One Corners to go to college and medical school, but there is a difference between you and me, Teal."

"What?" She sighed, knowing he had an infuriatingly plausible rebuttal.

"I wanted to come back."

"But living in a small town doesn't bother you . . . not like it does me."

"No, I've always loved our town," he said softly. "That's why I wanted to be a doctor. So I could come back to Thirty-One Corners and spend my life taking care of the people who took care of me."

"But you were always such a hell-raiser."

He grinned good-naturedly. "If all I knew about living was what I read in medical books, that would make me a very limited person, wouldn't it?"

"I help people—only in a different way," Teal reasoned, remembering all the fund-raisers she had catered.

"With little melon balls and fancy sandwiches?"

"What's wrong with 'little melon balls and fancy sandwiches'?"

"Nothing. Thirty-One Corners could use a good catering service."

Teal laughed. "For what? All the gala socials the Mettersons wish they could have?"

Bud didn't respond for a moment. "No, for all the ladies' bridge club luncheons, the hospital auxiliary luncheons, and Mayor Nelson's wife. Daisy Nelson could probably keep a catering service busy year-round."

Running her hand lightly down his chest, Teal asked softly, "Are you suggesting that I move my business to Thirty-One Corners?"

Her pulse raced. *What if he is? Would I consider doing it?*

He shrugged nonchalantly. "I just wondered if you'd ever thought about coming home."

"I don't know why it's suddenly so important for me to 'come home.'" Ceil had asked her that several times the past few days. "I've been gone for years. Thirty-One Corners isn't my home anymore . . . especially now that Uncle Carl and Aunt Winnie are . . ."

It was still hard for her to say "gone," but they were. They were gone, and this wasn't her home anymore.

"Maybe the town wants you back because the Anderson family is important to us."

"Us?"

Bud shrugged. "To everyone who knew Carl and Winnie."

"Winnie and Carl are gone." Teal had to blink tears back now.

"Yeah, but a big part of them lives on in you, Teal. Whether you like it or not, it always will."

• • •

It was late by the time they reached the farm. Bud carried the grocery bags and walked her to the door. The house was dark as they stepped up on the moon-drenched porch. "Ceil must have gone to bed early," Teal whispered.

"I'll call the garage first thing in the morning. They'll tow the Buick in and go over it tomorrow. It has probably been years since Carl had it serviced. He always insisted on doing everything himself. It's probably just a busted radiator hose," Bud said, putting down the bags, then leaning against the door jamb.

"Is that all? That's fairly simple, isn't it? The garage could have put a new one on in ten minutes."

"Yeah, I'm afraid they could have."

With her hand holding the key in the lock, she looked at him. "You mean this afternoon was all part of a sinister plan to be with me?"

"No, it was just pure luck that the hose blew, but I'll admit I took full advantage of the opportunity to have you to myself all afternoon."

"Oh, Bud." Her hand dropped to her side. "I really wish you wouldn't say things like that."

"Like what?"

"Like . . . anything personal could ever develop between us. It can't, you know. We're too different. . . . I escaped Thirty-One Corners once. I don't plan to come back."

"Escaped? Is that how you really see it?"

"Yes . . . no . . . I don't know. It doesn't matter. As soon as I find someone to finish out the harvest, I'm returning to Washington."

He reached out and smoothed a strand of hair

behind her ear. The intimacy of his gesture made her long to step into his arms.

"Why don't you hold on to the farm for a while? You don't need the money, do you?"

"I *won't* move back to Thirty-One Corners." She backed against the screen, feeling a touch of panic. He had a way of making her forget all the reasons she had left Thirty-One Corners. And if he continued to look at her in that sexy, loving way, he would have her wanting to go to another one of those dreadful John Philip Sousa concerts in Mettersons Park on Saturday night!

Sensing her fear, he straightened and pulled his hand away. "I've enjoyed the afternoon with you, Teal."

"Yes, so did I. Thank you for . . . everything."

"Anytime." Leaning forward, he brushed her lips with a light kiss, then turned and started down the steps.

Teal closed her eyes. *I will not fall in love with him. I will not,* she told herself.

She could hear the crunch of his boots as he walked back to his truck. He would be gone in two minutes. Two short minutes, and her crisis would be over.

Suddenly, she whirled and found herself shamelessly racing down the stairs. "Bud!"

Bud paused, his hand on the door handle of the truck. "Yeah?"

She ran up to him and hesitated for a moment, just looking up at him. She was out of her mind. She could not fall in love with him.

"Something you wanted?"

"Oh, hell!" she groaned. "In for a penny, in for a pound."

Stepping forward, she wrapped her arms around

his neck and brought his mouth down to meet hers. With a moan of male appreciation he caught her to him, his tongue meeting hers hungrily.

In that instant he realized that this was the moment he'd been dreaming of all these years, the day when Teal Anderson would take the first step and willingly, joyfully wrap her arms around him. To suddenly be in her embrace, to have her press against him, all warm, soft, and yielding, set his pulse racing. His breath caught in his throat as her lips traveled down his neck, flicking kisses light as butterfly wings inside his open collar while her slender fingers opened his shirt and fanned across his chest.

He closed his eyes, letting sensations shudder through him. He felt giddy, and a smile touched his lips at the irony of it all. He was the one who always made the moves, the one who always was in control, the one who always chose the time and the place, and here with a few surprises of her own was Teal intoxicating him with desire.

When had the tables turned? he wondered for a second, but his heart didn't care. He ran his fingers through her hair and gently tilted her head. "Come here, you," he said deep in his throat.

She lifted her lips to his with just a hint of a teasing smile, and he kissed each upturned corner before taking her mouth with full possession.

As he gathered her more tightly and deepened their kiss, tremors went rocking through her. Her heart pounded in her ears, sounding like a roar. As her knees weakened she sagged against him and held on for dear life, a part of her wondering if her trembling was being caused by Ceil's long-awaited earthquake. But as he lifted his head and looked down at her with unabashed hunger in his eyes, Teal realized that this quake was of the Bud Huntington variety, devastating to such a degree that she would not walk away unscathed.

Six

Help Wanted: experienced, responsible farm hand, until melon season ends. Must have references. Good pay.

Teal paid extra to have her newspaper ad set in bold type the second time it ran. She didn't know what a melon picker made, but she was willing to pay a dollar an hour more.

Her ad received a number of responses. In fact, Teal could hardly leave the phone the next Wednesday. By Thursday it seemed that every man in the three-county area had called "just to check out the job," but few seemed sincerely interested in overseeing what they called such a small patch, and even fewer were qualified when they came to talk to Teal on Saturday.

By the time she'd talked to the tenth applicant, she'd discovered that generous pay by her standards was low wages to the applicants. What they considered generous for picking melons was in her opinion nothing less than highway robbery!

Ceil had hovered on the back porch, naming

each applicant as he'd arrived and offering little tidbits of information about each.

"Bill Jordan. He's got a house full of kids and hardly stirs himself off the front porch. You don't want him."

Teal didn't.

"Carl Jacobs. His father-in-law keeps him under his thumb. So lazy you have to poke him with a stick to see if he's still breathing. You don't want him."

Teal didn't.

"Clyde Johnson. He drinks."

The smell of Scotch nearly bowled Teal over as she informed Clyde that the job was no longer available. Teal was practically wringing her hands when she heard Ceil exclaim, "Why, here comes Bill Brady. What's he doin' looking for a job?"

Bill wasn't looking for a job. Instead he said that he'd seen the realtor's sign and thought he'd stop by for a chat. Teal had a hunch that Bill was more interested in buying the farm for a song than he was in visiting, but she sat with him on the front porch, drinking lemonade and swatting flies until she thought she was going to die of boredom.

By the time Bill left, Teal was ready to tear her hair out in frustration. Another day gone, and she was no closer to finding someone to replace Mason than she'd been a week before.

That evening she returned to the hospital.

Mason's face brightened when she walked into his room. He was sitting in a chair by the window, his bony feet sticking out from beneath the hem of a striped bathrobe that had seen better days.

"How are you feeling?" Teal asked, pulling a chair up beside him.

"Fine as frog hairs," Mason assured. "And you?"

"Fine, but I have another question."

"Shoot."

"I've advertised for help on the farm."

"Yeah." His face fell. "Thought you might."

"I didn't want to, Mason. At first I thought I could handle the melons by myself, but there are a lot of melons out there." She sighed. "A whole lot."

Mason chuckled. "Yes, there's a whole lot of melons there, all right, little missy. Guess you didn't have much luck with the ad?"

Lifting her shoulders, Teal managed a faint smile. "I have to admit, I'm disappointed with the results. There's only one man whom I might consider. Harvey Wilson. You know anything about Harvey?"

Mason rested his head against the back of his chair, thinking. "Well, Harvey knows farming. Used to run a four-hundred-acre place in the next county—mostly soybeans, some rice. But, to be honest, I don't know why he'd be interested in a patch as small as Carl and Winnie's."

"He said that ordinarily he wouldn't be, but his wife's expecting another baby and he can use the extra money."

"Well now." Mason closed his eyes and Teal wasn't sure that he hadn't nodded off until he spoke a few moments later. "If a man needs the money, he'll most likely do a good job for you."

"Then Harvey's dependable?" Teal prodded.

"I would expect so. And he knows his melons," Mason admitted. "As well as anybody, I'd imagine. He should do."

Teal had been hoping that Harvey would come with a better endorsement, but at that point, the fact that "he should do" sounded pretty good. Besides, Harvey would be working only a few weeks, so if he was dependable, that was all that mattered.

"Well, thanks, Mason. You've been a big help." Teal patted his hand as she got up to leave. "You need anything? Books? Magazines? Candy? A wild woman?" she teased.

Mason waved her offers aside, ignoring the mention of a wild woman. "No, Doc and Thelma get me anything I need. You let me know if Harvey gives you any trouble. I'll straighten him up."

"Thanks. I will."

As Teal started to leave, Mason suddenly called to her, "You taking good care of Ceil?"

Teal turned and smiled. "Yes."

"She sure don't want to go to Mortwiler's, but you know that, don't you?"

"I know that."

"This earthquake thing has got her all flustered. Guess I'm going to have to hurry up and get well so's I can marry her."

Teal wondered if she'd heard him right. "Marry her!"

"Now, don't go telling *her* that, little missy! No use gettin' her all up in the air, since I don't know for sure that's what I'm gonna do. I just thought that you might want to know that I've been givin' the idea a little thought, that's all."

"Oh . . . no, no, I won't mention it to her."

"Well, just see that you don't," Mason grumbled. "No use gettin' her bowels in an uproar till we see how this health thing turns out."

"You'll be fine, Mason." Teal grinned, finding it difficult to believe that she was actually going to say her next words. "You've got a good doctor."

"Yeah, he's all right, I guess. Annoys the hell out of me, but I guess he knows his medicine."

As Teal slipped from Mason's room, she found herself hoping that Mason would marry Ceil. Knowing that Ceil and Mason would take care of each other would make it easier for her to return to Washington.

As she approached the elevator she heard someone calling her name.

"Teal? Teal Anderson?"

Glancing in the direction of the voice, Teal saw a woman about her own age hurrying down the corridor toward her.

"Teal?"

"Yes?"

"Hi, there! You probably don't remember me—I was three years ahead of you in school." The woman drew near and extended her hand in greeting. "I was so sorry to hear about Carl and Winnie's deaths."

"Thank you," Teal said, trying to recall the woman's name.

"I'm Connie Waters—Vinson now."

"Oh, sure. I remember you. You were head cheerleader my freshman year."

"That was me." Connie beamed. "Now I'm head of the Ladies Hospital Auxiliary. Listen"—Connie glanced around, trying to locate a corner where they could talk privately—" do you have a minute? I'd like to ask you something."

"Sure," Teal said, her curiosity aroused.

They strolled into a small lounge. Connie hadn't changed much. She was still a small, petite, perky blond who would probably always look youthful, even when she was sixty.

"Coffee?" Connie asked, pointing toward the vending machine.

"No, thanks."

"I know you must be wondering why I've dragged you in here."

Teal smiled, waiting for her to continue.

"The Hospital Auxiliary is having our summer luncheon next week, and I was wondering . . . well, Winnie talked so much about your catering business— would you consider catering our luncheon? It wouldn't have to be anything like those big Washington dinners you do, just something small but nice."

"Gee, Connie, I don't know. . . ."

"Oh, I know you're busy trying to close the farm, but I've heard so many wonderful things about your work. I thought since you were here, maybe you'd want to show off a bit, you know, show all these people what a star you've turned out to be?"

Teal laughed. "A star?"

"Well, sure. You're quite a celebrity in Thirty-One Corners. Most people around here have never left the state, let alone gone to Washington and socialized with all those senators and congressmen."

"I 'socialize' with very few senators and congressmen," Teal admitted, though she found the mistaken presumption flattering.

"Well, I know I'm asking a lot, but would you consider doing it for us? It would be a real treat for the Auxiliary."

Catering the luncheon might be fun, Teal thought. And it might feel good to be back in her element. She suddenly decided to do it. "I don't see any reason why I can't do your luncheon for you, Connie. Do you have a theme in mind?"

"Not really. I'll leave that up to you."

"Okay then, when is it?"

"This Friday, here in the boardroom. I'll tell the front desk, so you can come and go as you please."

Connie smiled broadly, obviously pleased with Teal's acceptance. "Oh, I'm just so relieved that you'll do this for us. Of course, we'll pay your regular fee."

As Teal stepped out of the elevator a few minutes later, she reminded herself that it was just one small luncheon. What could be the harm in catering one small affair? One ladies auxiliary luncheon couldn't threaten her decision to leave Thirty-One Corners. By the time she finished the project for Connie, Harvey would be acquainted with his duties, and she could leave.

Simple.

Harvey Wilson started work the next day.

Teal was stirring up a confectioner's mixture for miniature mints for the luncheon while keeping an eye on the field to make sure Harvey didn't collapse in the heat as Mason had done. Although Harvey was a good fifty-five years younger than Mason, Teal didn't want to press her luck.

By Friday she was as excited about the luncheon as Connie. And she had to admit that Connie had been a dream to work with. She hadn't screamed or demanded anything, and it was the first time in a long time that Teal hadn't had to live on aspirin prior to a luncheon.

Friday dawned hot and humid. Ceil helped Teal gather all the insulated coolers they could find around the farm and fill them with ice to keep the food cool until she got to the hospital. Connie had assured her that there was a kitchen next to the boardroom, complete with a refrigerator, so she could transfer the food there until it was time to serve.

After showering, Teal chose a white dress with a V neck and a wide flowing skirt for the occasion. She pinned her hair on top of her head and turned in front of the mirror, wondering if Bud would approve.

Bud. He was on her mind a lot lately. And chances were she wouldn't see him at all that day, so the dress didn't really matter. Still, she spritzed on an added touch of White Gardenia perfume just before she walked out the door.

By ten-thirty she was busy arranging platters in the hospital kitchen. For the first time since returning to Thirty-One Corners, she felt good about being there. She was finally doing what she did best.

By the time Auxiliary members began arriving, Teal was prepared. Everything looked exactly as she wanted.

"The tables are beautiful!" Connie exclaimed as she entered the kitchen carrying a large arrangement of colorful flowers.

"I'm glad you like them," Teal said with her head inside the refrigerator.

"We'll have lunch first, then our speaker will deliver his talk, then we'll have dessert—if that's all right with you?"

"Sounds good to me." Balancing a large bowl of fresh fruit, Teal closed the refrigerator with her hip. She glanced at the bouquet of flowers and wondered if Connie had misunderstood. She had ordered the fresh floral arrangements and already placed them on the tables.

"Looks like everyone showed up today," Connie remarked. "And are they ever going to be surprised when they find out that you're catering the lunch."

Teal smiled. "I'm happy to do it." Accustomed to

larger, more elaborate preparations, she found planning and preparing this affair a snap, but it was nice to have her work appreciated.

"By the way, these flowers are for you. They're from my garden. I thought you might enjoy having them," Connie told her as she set the bouquet on the counter.

"For me?" Teal turned, shocked that Connie would have brought her flowers. No client had ever brought her flowers.

"I cut them fresh this morning. Enjoy!"

Connie breezed out the doorway, leaving Teal to simply stare at the lovely bouquet.

The Auxiliary members began to gather in the boardroom, breaking off into small groups to chat. Teal returned to the kitchen to see to the last-minute details. She'd planned a simple buffet, and everything but the frosted apricots was set out.

As she arranged the fruit on platters she absently listened to the noisy babble, wondering when the conversation would get around to the earthquake. It didn't take long.

"Daisy, dear, how many water purification tablets do you think is necessary to keep on hand?"

"Why, I don't know, Geraldine. I keep four or five dozen. I don't want to be caught empty-handed, you know."

"Well, if you ask me, I think keeping a crowbar beside the bed isn't real bright. Frank got up in the middle of the night last night and stepped on it. Nearly broke his big toe, I tell you. My lands, the way he carried on a-cussin' and hoppin' around on one foot, you'd have thought he'd been mortally wounded," Nettie Johnson was telling Daisy Nelson.

"Well, isn't that the truth, Nettie? I told my

husband if the house caves in on us so bad we have to pry ourselves out with a crowbar, why, there's no telling what shape we'll be in," Daisy sympathized.

"Oh, I know it's foolish," Mildred Yarnell complained to Mitzi Millhouser. "Edward just couldn't believe that I would actually buy a gold chain to put my whistle on, but I just couldn't bear to wear it on that ugly old string around my neck."

"I know, dear, but wearing a whistle is important," Mitzi soothed. "If we're trapped in the house, we just blow the whistle and the rescue workers can find us easier."

Teal appeared from the kitchen carrying the platter of frosted apricots. With a whistle on a gold chain, Mildred Yarnell would be the best-dressed earthquake victim in Thirty-One Corners, she thought, then smiled appreciatively when the ladies recognized her and broke into delighted applause.

As the hands of the clock approached noon Connie suddenly broke away from one of the groups and clapped her hands for attention.

"Ladies, ladies! It's time to begin! Please take your seats!"

As Teal graciously accepted the accolades Bud stepped into the boardroom. Glancing at him, Teal felt color rising to her cheeks.

Lifting his brows in amused surprise, Bud nodded pleasantly at her as Connie caught his arm and edged him toward the center table.

"Ladies, oh, ladies! Our guest speaker is here!"

The ladies oohed and ahhed as they greeted the handsome young doctor.

Connie fussed over Bud a few more minutes, telling him how they were all eagerly looking forward to hearing his speech—"Bunions: Learning How to Cope."

After Connie hurriedly moved Bud into the buffet line, she flitted back and forth, making sure everything was moving smoothly. Teal had prepared quiche Lorraine, quiche Florentine, crab salad, an array of fresh fruit, pickled peaches, frosted apricots, and miniature tea rolls. She stood at one end of the table and continued to acknowledge the ladies' compliments with a sunny smile. She was keenly aware that Bud was approaching, plate in hand, his dark eyes focusing on her as he listened vaguely to the chatter and nodded at the appropriate times.

His gaze never left her as if she were the only woman in the room. Teal could feel her shoulders tensing and the butterflies swarming in her stomach. Her eyes flicked to others as they spoke to her but always returned to Bud. She tried not to look at him, tried to ignore his dark eyes, but her body bypassed her brain and instinctively turned in his direction.

When am I going to stop acting like a gawky adolescent every time he's around? Why is it I can be a polished professional only until he hits the scene?

Bud's brow creased in a frown when he seemed to notice that she was annoyed with his being there and even more annoyed that his presence made her so flustered.

The look in his eyes was so unsettling, so personal, that it made her feel as light as a feather in the wind.

If he doesn't stop looking at me like that, I am going to scream. He's toying with me, just like he does with his motorcycle when he revs it up.

He extended his plate toward her, and she took it automatically, their fingers brushing in the exchange.

"Maybe you could choose for me," he said, his gaze sweeping down her length and back up to her eyes. "Everything looks so good."

Teal started to shove his empty plate back into his hands until she heard Connie's voice. "Oh, do serve the good doctor. We want him to try everything you have."

Teal blushed, ignoring the light of growing amusement in Bud's eyes. She moved down the line, filling his plate hurriedly.

"Don't forget the peaches, Teal," Connie suggested. "I'm sure he'd love your peaches."

Teal reached across the table for the serving spoon. She glanced up and caught Bud's warm gaze drifting down the V neckline of her dress where it gaped open as she leaned over.

"Peaches—a real favorite of mine," he said, ignoring the bowl of fruit in favor of the view down her dress.

Teal straightened abruptly and spooned two pickled peaches onto his plate. Her face was blushing, her heart was pounding, and her hands were trembling. She had been serving food for years. Never had she felt so awkward and clumsy. The plate tilted slightly, and the peaches sailed to the rim. Bud's hand shot out to steady the plate, covering her hand in the process.

Her eyes met his across the table, and he could see her embarrassment. His face sobered, and he smoothly eased the plate from her hand.

"A beautiful table, Teal," he remarked. "My compliments."

Teal managed a polite nod before walking toward

the kitchen, muttering something about needing more ice.

Bud kept pace with her and veered toward her as she tried to duck past him.

She turned her head as his arm brushed hers. "What are you doing here?" she whispered, her irritation showing.

"I work here. Remember? What are you doing here?"

"Working." Her eyes were snapping fire as she turned her head and stepped into the kitchen.

Bud followed Connie to the head of the table with a hint of a smile on his lips.

The luncheon went smoothly. When it was time for Bud to speak, there wasn't a frosted apricot left. Teal saw Mildred sneak two into her purse to take to her husband, and Peggy Jordan snatched the last one and popped it into her mouth as she took her seat.

As Bud took the podium Teal disappeared into the kitchen to wash dishes, trying to keep a straight face. "Bunions: Learning How to Cope"— she could hardly wait to hear his lecture.

She stepped out of her shoes and listened to him gravely extolling the miseries and eventual acceptance of coping with bunions. Twice she nearly giggled aloud. The sheer agony of having to speak on the topic occasionally sifted through Bud's voice.

It was Teal's worst nightmare come true. Standing in a kitchen in Thirty-One Corners, barefoot, listening to Bud Huntington talk about bunions. Except this handsome, dynamic young hunk of a doctor was nothing like the Bud Huntington she'd been stuck with in her family living class all those years before.

When the enthusiastic round of applause signaled that Bud was finally about to escape, Teal stuck her head out the kitchen door.

With a smirk she waved, trying to attract his attention.

He glanced up from his conversation with Daisy Nelson, and his brows lifted questioningly.

Making a circle with her thumb and forefinger, she mouthed the word, "Awesome! Agony of 'De Feet'?"

He pretended to be thoroughly affronted as he folded his speech, jammed it into the pocket of his white coat, and with nose held high stepped off the podium and exited the room.

Speechless, Daisy watched him go, wondering what she had said that he taken the wrong way.

Teal was still grinning as she disappeared back into the kitchen.

Later, she was walking down the hallway carrying a box of dishes when she felt an arm circle her waist. The arm pilled her into an empty hospital room amid her protests.

"Shhh," Bud told her. "There are sick people in this hospital."

"People suffering with bunions?"

"Have you ever had a bunion?"

"Can't say as I have, but if I ever get one, I'll know to come to good ol' Doc "Bunion" Huntington," she teased.

He removed the box of dishes from her hands and set her down on the hospital bed. "You do that, Ms. Anderson. It would be my pleasure to treat your bunions or whatever else needs treating."

Before she knew what was happening, he'd sat down beside her and pulled her into his arms. As his mouth lowered to hers Teal drew back, but this time he didn't give her the option of retreat. His lips covered hers in a kiss that was exploratory at first, then filled with the urgency of long pent-up emotion.

Teal felt the heat ignite inside her. It was useless to fight. She was consumed by the same need she felt coursing inside him. It was foolish to deny it; more than that, it was dangerous. The more she disowned her feelings, the stronger they seemed to grow, until, as then, they swept out of control.

When their lips finally parted, Teal wrapped her arms around his neck, sighing. It was strange the way she kept falling into his arms, especially when she was supposed to be avoiding him.

"What was that for?" she asked.

"Damned if I know. Maybe I wanted to show my appreciation for . . . your peaches." His fingers traced a path down her neck and into her deep V-neckline. As he gently explored the mysteries there, he watched the color darken in her eyes.

"I beg your pardon," she managed to say hoarsely.

He kissed her again with a slow, leisurely patience. Teal knew it was crazy to let him go on, but everything about her life was suddenly crazy.

"Your talk was really quite good, Doctor. I was impressed," she admitted, dismayed to hear how shaky her voice sounded.

"And I was impressed with you." He lay back on the bed, looking at her. Lightly, he trailed his finger down the back of her arm, watching the goose bumps rise. "Your luncheon was elegant."

"Elegant?"

He bowed his head respectfully. "Everything was lovely, but I'm already hungry again." Leaning closer, he said softly. "You owe me a meal."

"Crybaby," she chided. "Besides, that was lunch. My dinners are more filling."

"I think a nice steak and baked potato would make up for all those frosted apricots." For a moment an awkward silence lay between them. Would she refuse to see him again? he wondered.

She released a long sigh, then turned her head to look at him. There was something unresolved between them, something that she was beginning to believe was inevitable. "How do you like your steak?"

"Medium rare."

She shrugged. "Medium rare it is."

"When?"

"When do you want?"

"Tonight."

Teal's face sobered slowly. "Bud . . . we're seeing a lot of each other lately."

"So?"

"So . . . I don't want you to think . . . I don't want you to assume that . . ." Her voice trailed off.

"I'm not assuming anything. We're two old school buddies having dinner together before you return to Washington."

Teal lifted her gaze to meet his. "Is that really how you see it?"

"Isn't that the way it really is?" His eyes searched hers, hoping he would find a hint of denial.

Gazing back at him, Teal knew that if she saw him again, it would be more than that. Much more than that. "I just don't want anyone to get hurt," she said softly.

"Nor do I. That's why we'll agree to keep it casual," he said lightly.

"I have to return to Washington," she said as if

she were reminding herself, not him. "I can't stay here, Bud. I can't fall in love with you—"

Laying his hand gently across her mouth, he stopped her words. "Just dinner, Teal, I'm not asking for anything more. I know how you feel about Thirty-One Corners, and though I wish you could feel differently, I understand."

But did he understand? Teal wondered, as his mouth lowered to take hers again.

Because if he did, she wished he would explain it to her.

Seven

"There you go, Mr. Greene. That should travel well."

"Thanks," the old gentleman said, picking up his box of tomatoes. "They look like dandies."

"They sure do."

As William Greene pulled out of the graveled area, Teal saw Bud's pickup pulling in.

She rolled her eyes when she saw the bright-red and white stock car in the trailer hitched to the back of the truck.

"Now, let me guess," Teal began as Bud approached the fruit stand. "You're on your way to make a house call, and you're taking the patient a stock car?"

"Wrong."

"You're on your way to the stock car races, where you intend to drive that . . . that thing yourself." Teal assessed the racing machine sourly.

"Right."

"You're nuts."

"And you're beautiful."

"And you're still nuts."

"Do you know you're the only person around here who talks to me like that? Most people address me with respect, like 'Dr. Huntington, how are you today?' or with friendliness, like 'Bud, good to see you! You're looking good,' but what do I get from you? 'You're nuts.' And you don't even soften it with '*Doctor*', you're nuts.'"

"Most people probably don't give a rip if you break your neck."

Winking, he flashed her a boyish grin. "And you do?"

Ignoring his remark, Teal busied herself with rearranging the melons. True to his word, Bud had kept their dinner the past week casual. They had talked, shared a bottle of wine, and enjoyed a delicious meal. When he'd walked her to the door around midnight and kissed her, the world had tipped—but only slightly.

"What time will you finish up here today?"

"I'm not sure. Most of the melons are gone, so I'll probably close the stand early."

"Then there's no reason why you can't go to the stock car races with me."

Stacking the last two melons in the bin, she fixed her gaze evenly on him. "I don't date men who drive stock cars. I don't even *like* men who drive stock cars."

"That's what you said about bareback bronc riders," he countered.

"And I meant it."

"What time can you be ready to go?"

She heaved a sigh. "Around two."

"I'll pick you up then." He leaned forward and gave her a promising kiss, one that made her wish that she had said around one.

. . .

Four hours later Teal sat in the bleachers surrounding an asphalt race track, her eyes riveted on the red and white stock car. Bud was positioned sixth in a field of twenty cars, their engines revving, waiting for the flag to fall.

The flag went down, and the cars roared into life.

Teal held her breath as she watched his car, the one with DOC painted on the top and the number 44 painted on the side, slide through the first turn.

The cars sped around the track, hitting one another, denting fenders, and crushing rear panels.

Teal closed her eyes and clutched her paper cup so hard that the contents flowed over the side. She wondered how she had ever let herself get talked into coming to this mess.

On the twenty-fourth lap 44 went into a skid. Teal nearly choked on a piece of ice as she shot to her feet, her eyes glued on Bud as he fought for control of the car.

She sat down abruptly and dropped her head, afraid to look.

Beside her a woman shrieked, "It's okay, honey! He made it!" as she energetically pounded Teal on the back.

Teal buried her face in her hands and listened to the roar of powerful engines and grinding metal.

The woman began jumping up and down, yelling and still pounding Teal on the back as the cars streaked down the straightaway for the final lap.

The white flag came out, and the crowd went crazy. A cup of ice came flying over Teal's shoulder as a man sitting behind her sprang to his feet, shouting, "Get on it eighteen!"

Teal opened her eyes a crack and saw that car 44 was in a duel for first place with car 18. Her heart hammering as loudly as the engines' roar, she watched the two cars battle around the first curve and head down the backstretch.

"Come on, forty-four!" the woman beside her shouted.

She turned to Teal, amazed to see that Teal had her hands over her eyes again. "How can you do that? Don't you want to see what happens?"

Teal shook her head. This was worse than the bronc riding!

The cars banged their way around the third turn and headed for the homestretch. The crowd surged to its feet.

Suddenly, Teal could stand the suspense no longer. Bounding to her feet, she began screaming at the top of her lungs, cheering the wildest kid in town to victory.

Car 44 shot across the finish line under the checkered flag.

"He won! He won! He won!" Teal jumped up and down and grabbed the woman standing next to her, and they pounded each other on the back. "He won!"

After car 44 came around the track and Bud accepted the checkered flag, the woman nudged Teal into the aisle. "Go down there and give him a kiss, girl!"

Teal pushed her way through the crowd and into the pit area. Bud was just pulling in as she ran down the long row of cars to meet him.

He climbed out of the car and pulled off his

helmet to see Teal approaching, breathless but all smiles.

He flashed her a grin, his face covered in dirt. "Hi, Ms. Anderson. Did I shake you up?"

"That was horrible!" she accused. "I thought you were going to be killed!"

He caught her to him and bent his head to kiss her. The crowd roared their approval.

Teal kissed him hard and hugged him tight, glad to have him back from the brink of disaster. His body felt warm and strong in her arms. Colors that rivaled a rainbow exploded behind her closed eyelids. His scent surrounded her, the scent of life lived to its fullest. As he reluctantly released her moments later, it occurred to her that this man did nothing in half measures, never had and never would.

It was after midnight by the time the car was loaded back on the trailer and Bud climbed into the truck.

"You really are nuts," Teal told him again, but there was more affection than accusation in her voice.

"You had fun, didn't you?"

"Yes and no." Her features softened as their gazes met in the moonlight. Yes, that night had been fun, but his hunger for excitement terrified her. That night only reinforced what she'd known all along. She was falling in love with him. Deeply in love. In spite of all she had vowed, she was in love with a man whom she couldn't possibly marry. She didn't fall in love with men who rode rodeo broncs and drove stock cars.

Marriage to a man like Bud would mean giving up everything she had worked so hard to acquire: her business, her independence, her freedom from

Thirty-One Corners. She wasn't prepared to make such a sacrifice, even if Bud could return her feelings.

They had shared some intimate kisses of late, but intimate kisses didn't ensure a lifetime commitment. She had to be practical. They were so completely wrong for each other. The contrast in their personalities was almost ludicrous. Bud liked to live on the edge, yet his roots were firmly planted in quiet, uneventful Thirty-One Corners.

She, on the other hand, loved the bright lights and the big city. Yet once her day was over, she looked forward to a quiet evening. What sort of relationship could she and Bud possibly hope to have with two such diverse personalities?

Yet Teal knew that her arguments fell lamely by the wayside when he flashed that carefree, devil-may-care smile at her. At those times she wasn't sure if she could live without him.

Riding back to Thirty-One Corners with the wind blowing through her hair gave her a sense of déjà vu. It was as if she had traveled back to a time when she used to lie in bed at night fantasizing what it would be like to be The Greek's girl. It had been like flirting with danger, seeing how close you could come to the fire without getting burned. Now, she was The Greek's girl—or she could be. Somehow she knew that.

It was after two when Bud pulled into her driveway and switched off the engine. Dawn and the harvesting of melons would come soon, but Teal was in no hurry to see the night end. It had been wonderfully exciting, and she wouldn't have wanted to miss it for anything.

Bud shifted sideways in the seat and smiled at her. "Penny for your thoughts?"

"I'd have to give back change," she admitted.

He ran his fingertips lightly down her neck, sending shivers down her spine. "Harvey working out okay?"

"He's doing fine. He says the melon season will be over in couple of weeks."

"A couple of weeks. That's not very long."

"No, not long."

He lowered his mouth to hers, savoring the feel of her lips, her taste, and wondering somewhere in the back of his mind how he would manage without her. She had touched his life in a way no other woman had.

"Teal, I wish you didn't have to go back to Washington," he said when the kiss ended.

His words hung heavily between them. At that moment she was beginning to think she didn't ever want to go back, and that frightened her even more than his kisses.

"Bud, please . . . you promised. Just old school buddies . . . remember?"

"I remember," he said quietly. "It's just hard to at times."

Settling into his arms, Teal gazed at the full moon and admitted to herself that she felt a sense of peace there that she had never felt before. "My work is in Washington, and my life is there, now. It isn't that I hate Thirty-One Corners," she whispered, aware of what he must be thinking. "The town is different now . . . much different," she conceded.

"Is the town different, or are you?"

Teal shook her head. "I'm not sure. . . ." She turned and gazed up at him. It was hard to conceal that she was feeling uncertain right then. Was it just the magic of his eyes in the moonlight, or was he *the* man she wanted to spend the rest of her life with? "I'm scared, Bud," she admitted, "and confused. Before I came back to Thirty-One Corners, I knew exactly what I wanted. Now, at times, I'm not so sure anymore."

Drawing her protectively to his chest, he held her and buried his face in her perfume-scented hair. "I'm scared too, Teal, because I know what I want, and it isn't life in a big city."

"Life in a big city isn't so bad."

"It would be for me." The light in his eyes grew tender. "Though it would be one hell of a choice to make, if I were ever asked to make it."

Because she could not promise more, she offered him her lips. Because he would not pressure her, he took her mouth with all the fervor of a man who wanted a lifetime but who would take each moment as it came.

Wallace Greer called late Wednesday morning to say that the final details of the estate were ready for completion.

The wills would be entered into probate, and as soon as the farm was sold, the estate would be settled. Wallace asked Teal to come to his office at four, and she agreed.

After Teal emerged from the attorney's office late that afternoon, she found herself wandering aimlessly down Main Street. Matters were taken care of now. She could book a flight back to Washington at the end of the week. She could call the storage company and have the furniture moved Friday morning. Mortwiler's was expecting Ceil, so there was nothing to prevent her from returning to Washington. Nothing except her feelings for Bud.

Funny, returning to D.C. didn't seem nearly as imperative as it had a few weeks earlier. How much of that had to do with Bud?

More than she wanted to admit, she realized. Much more than she dared to admit.

Her stomach growled, reminding her that she had missed lunch. Pausing in front of Wilson's Café, she smiled wistfully.

The café hadn't changed much over the years. The tables were still gray, and the booths red vinyl. The counter stools still swiveled, and if she wasn't mistaken, the menus were the same ones she'd ordered from as a child.

She went inside and slipped into an empty booth. She ordered a cheeseburger and a chocolate malt and looked out the window. The stores were closing for the evening, and people were going home, waving and calling to one another in a way that would never happen in a bigger city.

She watched as Fred Bowman flagged a car to a stop in the middle of the street. He leaned inside the window and talked to the driver for a few minutes before the car moved on. Nobody minded.

Comfortable. That was the word that came to mind. Thirty-One Corners wasn't exciting, but it was comfortable . . . and pleasant.

When she'd been growing up, the town had seemed dull, boring, and uninteresting, full of dull, boring, uninteresting people. Yes, the town had changed on the surface. The stores were a little nicer, a little more updated, but they were still the same stores run by the same people. The only major difference was that what she'd always thought was dull and boring wasn't really that at all. The people in Thirty-One Corners were easygoing and low-keyed. They took time to live instead of just reacting to the demands of society. They took time to talk to a friend. They took time to give comfort. She couldn't count the number of people who had attended Carl and Winnie's funeral and stopped by the farm for days afterward to leave food and flowers and kind words. Just thinking about it brought tears back to her eyes.

When she'd left twelve years ago, she had welcomed the thought of living in a place that offered choices—a choice of theaters, a choice of museums, a choice of restaurants.

Looking out at Main Street, she saw the town's one movie theater. No choices in Thirty-One Corners. But few conflicts either. No problem choosing a movie. Everyone saw what was playing that week.

And there was Spartan Drug. The soda fountain served only strawberry, vanilla, and chocolate. No thirty-three flavors to agonize over. Just strawberry, vanilla, or chocolate; single or double-dipped.

Instead of theater productions, there was bingo every Wednesday night at the VFW hall, where you sat elbow to elbow with your friends and neighbors and cheered each other on to win the big pot of the evening. And there was the square dance in the Legion hall on Saturday nights, with laughter, good times, and the best lemonade Teal had ever tasted.

No, Thirty-One Corners wasn't a glamorous place, but she could see why Winnie and Carl had been so content to live here.

Things were no different in Thirty-One Corners—what had changed was Teal Anderson.

• • •

As Teal left the restaurant thirty minutes later, she noticed that the Legion hall was all lit up. She could hear fiddle music coming from inside, and the laughter of men and women.

Curious, she stepped inside to watch. The dancers were whirling to the cry of Caleb Barnes, who had called square dances for over forty years. His body was stooped with age, but his voice was as strong as ever. His faded blue eyes danced with a pleasure that matched that of the dancers who moved at his bidding.

Footsteps were a blur and skirts were flying, revealing yards and yards of ribbon-trimmed petticoats as the dancers kept time to a rousing two-step.

Caught up in the gaiety, Teal stood in the doorway, tapping her foot to the music.

"Ladies to the right, gents to the left! Do-si-do, and don't let go!"

Teal's smile faded as she spotted Bud dancing with a pretty young brunette. The brunette was gazing up at him, her eyes worshiping him as he attempted to carry on a conversation above the music.

"That Sue Ellen Mosely is a real knockout, ain't she?" murmured a man who was standing next to her.

"Yes . . . Sue Ellen's a real knockout," Teal returned lamely.

With a jolt she realized that Bud had a private life. After all, he was the town's prize catch. Handsome, intelligent, successful, and single, he had it all. Bud Huntington was no longer the town's bad boy. He was a woman's dream come true.

Sue Ellen laughed as Bud leaned closer to say something to her. Jealousy welled up in Teal, immediate and powerful.

Fool. He's entitled to dance with anyone he chooses. He's entitled to do anything he wants with anybody he chooses. Like Bud said, a few kisses, a few casual dates, that's all we shared. Just two old school buddies having a good time before one of them returned to Washington. I'm the one who's taken the past few weeks too seriously, not Bud.

After Friday she would never see him again. That realization hit Teal like a brick wall.

Bud looked up. Spotting Teal, he waved.

Teal's heart turned over. After Friday she would never see him again.

She lifted her hand and waved back, then hurried out the front door.

She rushed down the sidewalk, tears burning her eyes. "You fool," she muttered. "You *have* fallen in love with him. Now what? Admit it, and be stuck in Thirty-One Corners for the rest of your life?"

Would that be so bad?

She didn't know. She wasn't sure of anything anymore.

Bud's voice interrupted the fierce dialogue going on inside her head. "Where are you going in such a hurry?"

"Home." She kept walking, aware that Bud was directly behind her. She couldn't let him see her crying!

"What's your hurry? There's no melons to pick tonight."

"I have pickles to move."

"The earthquake isn't predicted until December."

"Well," she said, tasting salty tears as she walked faster, "you never know. It can always come early, and it would be senseless to waste all those pickles Winnie worked so hard to—"

"Forget the damn pickles." Bud grabbed her arm and turned her around to guide her back in the direction of the Legion hall.

"Let go of my arm, Bud. I'm tired and I want to go home."

She was sure she looked like a mess, with mascara running down her cheeks and her nose rivaling Rudolph's in redness.

"I want to dance with you."

"Looks to me like you have a dancing partner," she accused, hating the hurt seeping through her voice.

"But she isn't you."

He steered her into the hall, and Teal balked, whirling to face him. Their eyes locked stubbornly. "Let me go, Bud."

"One dance, Teal. Then I'll take you home."

Taking her by the hand, he led her onto the dance floor as the band struck up a slow waltz.

He drew her into his arms. Held tightly against his chest, she found it impossible to think about anything except the scent of his after-shave and the warmth of his cheek resting lightly against hers. The fight slowly drained out of her.

"This is so hard," she admitted brokenly.

"Maybe, but it's harder for me not to say the things I want to say to you," he whispered.

"Maybe you should say them. Maybe . . . I need to hear you say them. I'm so confused."

"About what?"

About everything I've been feeling.

"About me?"

"Yes. Oh, Bud, is it just me . . . or *is* there something going on between the two of us? Something . . . warm and exciting and scary . . ."

He held her closer, and his breath sent shivers down her spine as he whispered in her ear, "I'm willing to explore the possibility if you are." She melted against him. "Stay with me tonight, Teal. Let me say all the things I want to say to you. Let me make love to you."

Her footsteps faltered as she looked up at him, but the moment was shattered when the call changed and she was suddenly whisked out of his arms by another dancer.

Looking at each other from across the room, they moved around the floor with other partners, but their thoughts were hanging on her unspoken answer.

For the next hour Teal danced with several partners. Her mind reeled with Bud's proposal. She had never in her life just gone off and spent the night with a man—but she had never in her life been in love.

Finally, she begged off from yet another partner and slipped outside. On the porch she paused for a breath, but it caught in her throat at the sight of Bud leaning negligently against the railing, arms crossed, watching her, waiting.

"As I was saying, if I don't make love to you, I am going to die."

A new light entered her eyes, one of love and, as much as she hated to admit it, surrender. "Well, I've never been fond of funerals."

"My motorcycle or your car?"

"I'm feeling reckless. Your motorcycle."

He stepped forward and brushed his lips lightly across hers. "Hold that feeling."

Five minutes later her skirt was hiked up to her thighs and she was holding on tight to Bud as they roared toward the city limits.

They couldn't talk over the roar of the motorcycle, but she didn't want to talk. And she didn't want to think. She just wanted to open herself to the sensations of the night, the wind whipping her hair, the moon rising, the stars sparkling in the midnight sky—and the feel of Bud.

Teal had no idea where he was taking her until he pulled in front of her house. Fortunately, Ceil was away for the night, or she'd have been out on the porch with a shotgun.

"What are you laughing at?" Bud asked as he helped her off the motorcycle.

"I was thinking it's a good thing Aunt Ceil is keeping Mildred company tonight, or she'd swear the earthquake had just struck."

"So will you." He lifted her into his arms and carried her up the steps.

"Oh, yeah?"

"Oh, yeah," he murmured suggestively against her mouth.

Teal elbowed the screen door open as their kiss deepened. Bud carried her through the doorway and made his way to her bedroom. Gone were the teenage years when he'd tossed pebbles at her window just to annoy her, but the location of her room was still fixed in his mind.

"You're sure Ceil's not home?"

"Positive."

He lowered her gently to the bed and began to remove his clothes, his eyes never leaving hers.

Teal watched each item fall away. Moonlight

spilled through the open window to highlight the ridges and contours of his strong, masculine body. There had been a time when she would have believed this was wrong, but over the past weeks a tide of tenderness and passion had surged between them until this moment seemed inevitable. The future was uncertain, but she was sure of one thing: She loved Bud Huntington.

The scent of honeysuckle floated on the breeze that lifted the curtains and stirred the wispy curls around her face.

As he tossed his shirt aside her hands came up to slide through the mat of dark hair that spread out in a thick V from the center of his chest.

He looked into her eyes and this time it wasn't hard for her to read his thoughts. "Maybe you would have liked to do this for me?"

"Maybe later," she said as her fingers moved to the top button on her blouse. It was time to reveal to Bud Huntington the woman she had become.

"Yeah," he whispered as he eased down beside her. "Definitely, later." His eyes darkened as he watched her open her blouse. When she paused after undoing the last button, he saw a shyness in her eyes that at once surprised and moved him.

His gaze moved to her mouth, and he brushed gentle kisses over her lips until he felt them yield and part. His tongue probing lightly with evocative thrusts, he felt her tension melt and her body settle easily onto the old quilt. He nibbled on her slender throat, which glistened like pale satin in the moonlight, pausing to trace a lazy circle where her pulse throbbed. When she released a sigh and murmured his name, he brought his mouth to hers with fierce longing.

Her fingers joined his as they peeled away her

clothes. For a moment he hovered over her, letting his gaze wander the lush hills and valleys of her body.

"You are so beautiful," he whispered.

"I was hoping you would think so," she said, her confidence growing with the warm look of pleasure on his face. She was sure of herself in matters of business, but this was a matter of intimacy, and it was unfamiliar territory.

"You're lovelier than I'd even imagined. And, believe me, I've imagined this moment for a long time."

A smile touched her lips. "So have I."

She reached for him, and his hands moved over her, working their magic. She felt a heat flare inside and soften like melted candle wax.

Her silky touch, her pliant curves, and encouraging murmurs mingled together to drive him to the edge. He fought for control, struggled for restraint while his hammering heartbeat blotted out all sound. His mind floated in a sea of colors, and he was surrounded by the sweetness of flowers and her.

She lifted her arms to draw him down inside her. Slowly at first, then with a quickening tempo, they fell into a rhythm, timeless and sure, until at last they topped the summit and plummeted joyously, tangled together, body and soul.

Eight

"Wake up, sleepy head, we've got a date with a catfish."

Teal groaned and forced her eyes opened. "A *catfish*?"

She honestly didn't like men who woke up at the crack of dawn, rode motorcycles, drove stock cars, and tried their best to kill themselves on bucking broncos. And she really didn't date men who went fishing at five o'clock in the morning.

She didn't even like men who went fishing at five in the morning. But she had to admit that she was deeply in love with one particular man who did all those things and who was seductively nibbling at her ear then while his hand gave her the most heavenly back rub.

Bud rolled her onto her back, and his mouth took hers in a long, earth-moving good-morning kiss.

"Is it the earthquake again?" she murmured.

"I think so," he murmured back, before kissing her deeply again.

"The wrench to turn off the gas line is under the kitchen sink. No, under Ceil's bed. No, wait, I don't know where it is. . . ." Her voice trailed off as they rolled deeper beneath the sheets, his hands making her lose her train of thought.

"Ummmm, this I like," she admitted against his lips. He smelled good, like soap and spicy aftershave. "But I'm not so sure about the catfish."

"Could I tempt you with apple pancakes and sausage links?"

"Apple pancakes? That would help," she admitted.

"Deal. After we catch a fish."

"We?" Her eyes opened slowly to see a wicked grin curving his lips. The devilment dancing in his dark eyes convinced her that he wasn't kidding. He actually expected her to go fishing with him. "I'm *not* going fishing."

"Yes, you are."

"Bud!"

"Teal!" he mocked, then pulled her back to him for another long, thoroughly debilitating kiss.

"Or I could be just as content to stay here and make love to you until the sun comes up," he said a little later.

"Ummm, you could, huh?"

His hand slipped beneath her T-shirt to cradle her breast. "No, on second thought, I sure do love the feel of a big old catfish pulling on my line."

"Oh really?" For the next half hour she devoted her time to making him think twice about his fish.

"Where are you going fishing?" she murmured later as they lay watching the room grow lighter.

"*We* are going fishing at the rice pond." His dark eyes captured hers, sending a tingle down her arms.

"Rice pond?"

He chuckled and smoothed hair out of her eyes. "You have forgotten a lot about Thirty-One Corners, haven't you? Best fishing around here is in the rice ponds."

Teal vaguely recalled the area near the farm where dirt had been removed to create a terraced levee. Carl had taken her fishing there when she was a child.

"Oh, yes. The rice pond. How could I forget?"

"Yeah, how could you? Rise and shine, woman. Fish bite best before sun-up."

Teal groaned, but he was already trying to untangle her from the sheets.

"Don't you have to work today?"

"No, and I want to get as far away from a telephone as I can get."

Pulling her to her feet, he drew her against his masculine length for another long kiss, then pointed her in the direction of the bathroom. Groaning again, she took a few steps and bumped sleepily into furniture as she went.

"Going fishing at this hour. Honestly . . ."

She stepped into the shower, and a few minutes later the curtain was drawn aside and a cup of coffee magically appeared.

Teal scrambled to cover herself with the washcloth and frowned at the man who leaned against the stall, his gaze openly admiring her.

"Don't tell me you're modest." The way his eyes refused to leave her body embarrassed her. As a matter of fact, she was modest. Painfully modest. And the nearly indecent way he was sizing her up didn't make her shyness any easier to overcome. "I don't like having an audience when I shower," she said simply.

"You'll get used to it."

He ducked as she pitched a soggy washcloth at him.

"Want me to wash anything? I won't look unless you tell me I can." He chuckled wickedly as he hastily sidestepped the bar of soap she tossed next.

"Go away!"

With a smile he pulled the curtain back in place, but he had no intention of going away.

Not when it came to her.

To Teal's credit it was an admirable fifteen minutes later when she entered the kitchen, dressed and ready to go.

"That does it, I'm in love." Bud handed her a piece of buttered toast to tide her over until they returned.

Teal broke the bread in half and took a bite. "With me?"

"With any woman who can shower and be dressed in fifteen minutes."

"You're too cheery for this hour of the morning," she complained as she walked to the refrigerator to pour herself a glass of milk. She really wished he wouldn't say that he was in love with her unless he meant it.

Of course, it was possible that he wasn't teasing. After the previous night, she found that thought very appealing. Though what she had done was still a mystery to her. Very few men had shared her life, even fewer had interested her to the point that she would have considered going home with them. Carl and Winnie's firm moral teachings had not been lost on her. She didn't enter a relationship with a man indiscriminately, so the fact that Bud Huntington could make·her forget all that she'd held sacred worried her.

Bud grinned, almost as if he'd read her thoughts. "You'll find out that I'm just cheerful by nature."

"Right. By the way, you need a haircut." Teal downed the milk and rinsed the glass.

"By the way, don't get bossy on me—not until I tell you you can."

"And when will that be?"

"When I tell you you can." Helping himself to another kiss from her, he put a fishing pole into her hand.

"Where on earth did you get this?"

"Madam, while you slept like a log, I showered, dressed, ran three miles, then drove to my house to get the fishing gear." He nudged her toward the door, anxious to be on his way. "I thought you'd never get up."

"It's five-thirty!"

"Exactly my point, I thought you were going to put roots in the bed."

"You and I would never make it if we were married," she complained as he urged her outside.

"Is that a proposal?"

"It is not."

"Good." He grinned. "I don't want you to get the idea I'm easy."

Fifteen minutes later the pickup pulled onto the levee.

Carrying two poles and a tackle box, Bud led the way to the pond. Teal, still yawning, followed behind with a thermos of coffee and a blanket.

Mornings began much later in Washington.

The sun came up slowly, bathing their surroundings with a satiny, mellow light. Teal sat on the bank, drinking coffee and savoring the quiet serenity of the pond. The only sounds were the plop of bait landing in the water and the birds' noisy chatter as they awakened to greet the new day.

She lay back on the blanket and studied the shifting clouds. The pale blues, pinks, and yellows created by the rising sun were striking. A small bank of slate-gray puffs were forming on the low horizon, and Teal wondered if they were a threat to the beautiful morning.

She lowered her gaze and watched Bud as he played his line, the muscles across his back stretching his shirt. He was a fine specimen of a man, in superb shape, athletic, taut, strikingly male. The cockiness of his youth had disappeared, replaced by a quiet, unassuming confidence that she found attractive. Twelve years before she'd never have imagined she'd actually be sitting by a pond, with The Greek nearby, fishing—

The Greek!

Bolting upward, she suddenly remembered the horoscope she'd read on the bus.

Beware of Greeks bearing gifts.

At her abrupt movement Bud glanced over his shoulder and frowned. "Something wrong?"

"No . . . nothing." Lying down again, Teal stared up at the sky. *What had she done?*

As a teenager she had fantasized about what it would be like to date Bud, but every girl in school had fantasized about him at one time or another, some more openly than others. No one could have missed the adoration in the girls' eyes when he'd walked down the hall wearing his black motorcycle jacket with his dark hair slicked back like a young Tom Cruise.

At that time Teal had prided herself on rising above the juvenile surge of hormones. She'd spent her energy on making good grades so she would be assured of a college scholarship. That scholarship had been her only way out of Thirty-One Corners, and she hadn't allowed herself to be distracted by a boy with dark eyes and black hair and a smile that would melt cement.

And you can't let yourself be distracted now. Teal. Last night was close to perfect, but it was just one night. You've worked hard to get where you are. If you gave in to a crazy notion and actually moved back, it would be only a matter of months before you realized what a mistake you'd made. Last night was nice, but it wasn't reality.

"Hey, I hope you're not planning on the fish coming to you," he called.

"I'm accustomed to having my fish delivered to my door, cleaned, and packed in ice," she returned lazily.

"Sorry, sweetheart, it doesn't work that way in Thirty-One Corners."

"Bud."

"Yeah?"

"Why haven't you ever married?" Teal knew her question was coming right out of left field, but it suddenly seemed important that she know.

He glanced up and his brows lifted mockingly. "Who wants to know?"

"I want to know."

"Any particular reason?"

"No . . . just wondering."

He threw his line out again, watching as it

settled into the water. "I've never met anyone I wanted to marry. How about you?"

"Most men are jerks."

"Waiting for me, huh?"

She laughed. "Yeah, really."

Their eyes met, and she noticed that the twinkle in his was suddenly gone. "I'm all yours. Come and get me."

"I'll be right there."

They gazed at each other in the morning sunlight, each trying to decide who was bantering and who was serious.

Bud was the first to break eye contact. Glancing up at the sky, he sighed. "Looks like it's going to rain."

His pole suddenly dipped, and he let out a whoop as a large fish broke the surface of the pond.

Teal jumped to her feet and clapped enthusiastically as Bud reeled the fish to shore.

"I'm impressed!" she cried.

"We have fish for dinner tonight!"

Teal laughed. "Only if you're offering to cook," she remarked.

"Only if you're offering to make the hush puppies," he added.

"It's a deal!"

The dark clouds that had been steadily rolling in decided to fulfill their prophecy. Rain began to fall, gently at first, but the sharp clap of distant thunder promised an imminent downpour.

Bud handed the fish to Teal, who wrinkled her nose and quickly dropped it into the wicker basket.

Another crack of thunder sounded as Bud hurriedly gathered up the poles and blanket. He grabbed her hand and they made a mad dash for his truck.

The sprinkle turned into a cloudburst, soaking them both to the skin. The truck was within sight when the wicker basket slipped out of Teal's hand.

"Wait! I dropped the fish!"

Lunging for the basket, Bud lost his footing. His feet flew out from under him, and he went down in a flurry of mild epithets.

Teal started laughing, though she knew that she shouldn't. Falling down wasn't funny, and yet he made a hilarious sight, sprawled out in the mud—or it seemed hilarious until her feet abruptly flew out from under her and she felt herself falling. She sprawled forward and screamed as she toppled headfirst on top of him.

Her struggle to get to her feet in the mud took her breath away, and she was laughing so hard that it was impossible to regain her balance.

Bud didn't find it so humorous. It might have had something to do with the fact that her weight kept shoving his face in the mud. She tried time after time to stand up, only to dissolve into laughter and fall back on top of him again.

"Teal, my face is buried in mud," he sputtered, not the least bit amused. "Get up."

"I can't . . ." She was mortified. She was not the giggly type, but the harder she tried to get up, the funnier it seemed, and the deeper his face got buried into the muck.

He grabbed her hips and heaved her aside, then struggled to his feet. She tried to stand up and fell sideways, taking him down with her again.

Spitting mud, she scrambled to her feet as he struggled back to his. They both looked at each other and broke into laughter.

"You're a city girl if I've ever saw one," he accused. "Have you forgotten how to get in out of the rain?"

She grinned, nodding.

"Well, if you think wallowing around in the mud is funny, you're going to get hysterical now."

She giggled. "Why?"

He nodded toward her feet.

She glanced down and saw that she was standing ankle deep in thick gumbo that stuck to her.

"Egad!" Her hilarity died a swift death when she tried to pry one foot loose only to succeed in burying the other foot deeper. Finally, both her feet were coated with so much muck that they weighed at least twenty pounds each.

Bud stood by, watching her efforts and chuckling to himself.

"It's not funny! Give me a hand!"

With an infuriatingly straight face he lifted his hands and clapped.

"Very funny. Now help me out of here!"

She looked so pathetic that he finally relented and lifted her. For a moment he held her up in the air.

"You look like some little hothouse flower that's been pulled up by the roots."

"Oh, yeah?" She grabbed him around the neck and kissed him, smearing his face and mouth with mud from hers.

He swore under his breath, then leaned over and spit out a mouthful of mud.

"Gee, I just love fishing! I never realized the *fun* I've been missing." Teal wiped the rain out of her eyes and grabbed his hand. Together they started toward the truck again. There was no hurry then.

When they reached the truck, Bud lowered the

tailgate and lifted Teal to sit on it. The initial cloudburst had passed, leaving a steady, gentle rain.

"You need to strip out of your clothes," he said as he tried to scrape mud off her shoes.

"I'd be naked."

"And I'd be happy."

"Bud, I can't strip out of my clothes," she chided. She had done some crazy things lately, but running around in the woods buck naked wasn't going to be one of them.

"Then I'll take them off for you," he said, his hand sliding up her calf.

Teal's gaze met his and suddenly their light-heartedness disappeared. In its place was the memory of the passion they'd shared the night before.

As if he'd read her mind, Bud stepped between her jean-clad thighs and cupped her face in his hands. His lips were warm and firm as they met hers. "Let's go back to the house," he whispered.

Soon they were back at the farm shedding their clothes. Laughing, they hopped into the shower together and thoroughly soaped away the mud.

Later, she lay beside him, idly tracing the path of his bare spine. Her stomach growled, reminding her that they should have had breakfast hours ago.

"I heard that," Bud mumbled into his pillow.

"If I remember, you promised me apple pancakes."

"Only if you were a good sport."

"I think getting rain-soaked and mired in muck—without complaint, mind you—classifies me as a good sport."

Bud sat up and kissed her again. "You're right. Apple pancakes coming up—at Wilson's Café."

"Wilson's Café! I thought you were fixing them."

He looked at her, unyielding. "*I* can't cook. My special apple pancakes are bought at Wilson's Café."

While Teal got into clean clothes, Bud retrieved his from the dryer. It was already noon when they arrived at Wilson's Café.

"I hope they serve breakfast any time of the day," Teal said as they got out of the truck.

"If they don't, we'll make them."

Later, when they climbed back into the cab of the truck, they were full and content.

Teal shrugged. "I should stop by the travel agency and book my flight back to Washington." The words were out before she realized what she was saying.

A quietness settled over the cab as Bud started the engine. "The agency doesn't close until late afternoon. You have plenty of time." Making a U-turn on Main, he headed the pickup out of town.

"Where are we going?" Teal murmured, scooting closer to him.

He slipped his arm around her and said quietly, "There's something I want to show you."

They drove for a while. Teal figured they had to be several miles out of town when the pickup turned down a rutted lane. At the end of it was a deserted house, nearly stripped of paint, its front porch sagging.

"Where are we?"

"This is where I grew up," Bud said, switching off the engine.

They sat in the silence for a moment, enjoying the tranquillity.

"It's a beautiful setting," Teal noted.

Bud shrugged. "I was never able to see that when I was growing up."

"I never knew where you lived."

"I didn't want you to know."

Teal turned to look at him. "Why?"

"I don't know. . . . Maybe I just never thought I was good enough for you."

"Oh, Bud." She laid her head against his shoulder, wishing he didn't feel the need to be so candid. "Why would you ever think that?"

"I don't know. . . . Because you were always so . . . classy, I suppose."

"Classy? Aunt Winnie and Uncle Carl never had anything."

"Not classy in that way, just . . . above me."

"I never meant to give you that impression."

"You always avoided me."

"I was always scared of you. Aunt Winnie warned me about boys like you," she teased.

"I used to lie in bed at night and wonder what kind of man you would marry. I knew it wouldn't be a man like me. I didn't have anything and didn't have much hope of getting anything. I pictured you in a big city with a rich husband, a big house, an expensive car, and two point five children—you know, the average family."

"Yeah." She sighed. "And here I am, back in Thirty-One Corners with not the slightest prospect of a rich husband, a big house, or my two point five children."

He looked at her, and Teal had the oddest feeling he was about to offer to change all that for her. But the moment passed, and he looked away.

Cuddling closer to him, Teal closed her eyes and forced back the rising lump in her throat. Had he been about to ask her to marry him? Would she have been foolish enough to refuse him?

Bud leaned against the door, staring out the windshield at the house that had once been his home, one hand resting on the steering wheel, the other resting on the window. The rain had brought the temperature down a few degrees, and a light breeze came through the open window, bringing with it the fragrance of the river and the open fields beyond it. Teal waited, aware that he was wrestling with a decision.

He finally released a long sigh. "When you came back to Thirty-One Corners, I thought I was over you."

"Bud, don't."

His eyes met hers, and she wasn't sure what she saw in them. Anger? Hope? Despair?

"Why?" His voice was ragged. "Am I still not good enough for you?"

"No. And it makes me angry that you would think that."

"Then what is it? I'm respectable. I'm not rich, but I'm not poor. And I love you, Teal. I don't just love you, I'm in love with you. I've never told a woman that before. I've never met a woman who makes me alive the way you do."

"Bud, please . . . it just won't work. . . ."

He turned to face her, his face sober. "Come home, Teal. Come home, and let's explore the possibility of a future together. I won't push you. I'll give you all the time you need."

She almost stopped breathing. "Don't," she pleaded again softly.

Hurt clouded his eyes. She could see his defenses rise, and she wanted to tear them down, but at what expense?

"Bud . . ."

He looked away.

"It isn't what you think." She reached for his arm to keep him from starting the truck. "It's not that I don't love you. I do."

"Then what's the problem?"

"Our lives are the problem, Bud. You've built a practice, a life here in Thirty-One Corners. My life is in Washington, D.C. I have a business there. A business I've neglected far too long."

"Your life in D.C. is more important than us?"

"Bud, there can't be an us. I *need* stability, security. You need danger and excitement; I would go crazy worrying about you. I'd live in fear that you're going to break your fool neck. I'd nag you to stop driving that darn stock car and riding those darn broncos and I hate fishing! We'd end up fighting all the time. We'd grow to hate each other."

"You place so little trust in our love that you think all these problems couldn't be worked out?"

"I *know* how they would be worked out. You would want me to move back here and be a silent, obedient, understanding wife."

"I haven't asked you to marry me." He turned the key and the engine rumbled to life, abruptly ending the conversation.

"There's no need to get angry about it," Teal protested lamely.

"I'm not angry. I asked you to stay and try to work things out, and you said no."

"I didn't say no."

"Did you say yes?"

"No. . . ."

"Did you say you'd think about it?"

"No. . . ."

"Then consider the subject closed."

"Well, great. That's just great!" She scooted away, feeling angry too. He was being unreasonable. She hadn't immediately agreed to move back to Thirty-One Corners, but she hadn't completely ruled out the prospect, either.

They drove back to the farm in a heated silence.

Teal groaned when she saw the Electra setting in front of the house. That meant that Ceil was home, and Teal's heart sank even farther. There was no way she could get into the house without Ceil's knowing that something was wrong.

If Bud's truck spinning gravel out of the drive didn't give it away, the tears Teal couldn't control surely would. And the last thing she needed now was a lot of questions that she couldn't answer.

Bud's truck skidded to a stop behind the sedan. Teal sprang out and slammed the door.

"If you should change your stubborn mind, let me know," Bud snapped.

"How? The subject is closed."

Teal marched toward the house, fuming. She hoped that he didn't plan to hold his breath until she changed her mind.

It would be a cold day in Hades before she would marry a man with that kind of temper!

Nine

"I still say you should go after him. Look at me, I'm not giving up on Mason and he's got one foot in the grave."

"Mason doesn't have one foot in the grave. The hospital said he's feeling better since the balloon surgery."

"Well, I still think you ought to go to the hospital and get this thing straightened out with Bud. He's a prize catch, you know. There's a lot of women in Thirty-One Corners who'd—"

"Aunt Ceil, I don't want to talk about it," Teal insisted for the tenth time that evening.

Ever since Bud had gunned his truck down the lane the previous night and left Teal standing in a cloud of dust, Ceil had persisted in questioning Teal's judgment, if not aloud, then under her breath.

Teal had refused to say what had happened, but that didn't mean Ceil wasn't astute enough to know something was wrong. Ceil admitted that she had always hoped that Teal and Bud would get together one day. But her hope for that was fading. Oh, there had been a brief flicker when Morleen Majors had called to say that she'd seen Teal and Bud dancing together at the Legion hall. According to Morleen, they had been cozying up real good. *Real* good. But it didn't take a genius to figure out that something must have gone wrong, and it was clear that Teal wasn't about to say what it was.

"I've moved the earthquake survival kit back under the stairs. That appears to be the best place for it after all," Ceil said. "If we're home when the shaking starts, then we can go right to it. If we're not, well, don't guess it'll matter anyway."

"Don't guess so," Teal agreed absently. She'd called the travel agency earlier and reserved a seat on a four o'clock flight to Washington the next day. She should be happy she was finally going to leave Thirty-One Corners, but at the moment, it didn't matter. Not a whole lot did matter—and not because of some earthquake that might or might not happen.

"Morleen said she saw you at the dance two nights ago."

"Oh?"

"Had a good time, huh?"

"It was okay." Teal stared out the kitchen window at the nearly empty melon patch. The season would be over in another week or two. She was only mildly surprised to realize that the thought disturbed her.

"The donkey kicked over the outhouse," Ceil said.

"I know," Teal responded without interest.

"And Mason Letterman asked me to marry him."

"That's nice."

"But I told him Ronald Reagan asked me first and that I couldn't disappoint him."

Teal glanced up. "What?"

Ceil sat across from Teal, her elbows on the table. "I wondered just where your mind had wandered. Now, tell me what happened? Bud roared out of here last night like his tail was on fire."

Not his tail, his heart, Teal thought wearily. *I hurt him, and myself, and I didn't set out to do that to either one of us.*

"Bud and I didn't see eye to eye on a discussion we were having."

"Oh. Could it possibly be a lovers' tiff?"

Tears brightened Teal's eyes as she turned away from the window, determined to shift the subject from Bud Huntington. "Did Mason really ask you to marry him?"

"Would I lie about a thing like that? Lord knows I've worked hard enough to get him around to asking. Course he did. Right there in the recovery room, in front of the nurse and all those other people."

"And you agreed."

A cagey look entered Ceil's eyes. "Well, I told him I'd think about it. I don't want him to think I'm overeager, you know. I could always go and live with my friends at Mortwiler's."

Teal smiled, turning to gaze out the window again. *As if she couldn't wait.*

Sighing, she thought about love and how nice it could be with the right man. She had waited for Bud to call all day, but he hadn't. Undoubtedly, he realized that the relationship was as hopeless as she'd known all along. Still . . .

"Why don't you marry Bud? I'll marry Mason,

and we'll make it a double wedding," Ceil suggested.

"A relationship between Bud and me would never work," Teal murmured. "We're entirely different people."

"Well, I should hope so. Isn't that the way it's supposed to work? Good lands, Teal. If you love the man, go after him. Things have a way of working out if two people really love each other." And Ceil had a way of simplifying the most complex of problems, Teal thought. If only her problem could be that easily solved.

"Aunt Ceil, I don't want to talk about it," she repeated firmly.

"Don't surprise me none. You always were good at keeping things to yourself." Ceil slid out of the booth and shuffled across the room to put her glass in the sink. Teal noticed that Ceil wasn't moving as fast as she usually did. "Well, I think I'll go watch Arsenio before I go to bed. He's always good for a laugh, and I could use one." She yawned, then stretched wearily. "It's like Kinderson Funeral Home around here tonight."

She started down the hall, her voice fading as she went. "That Mildred called me today and near talked me half to death. You'd think she hasn't seen a soul in weeks, but I know for a fact that old Gilbert Wadslow checks on her every day. If you ask me, I think Gilbert's got a thing for Mildred. Of course, she swears up and down that I'm just makin' that up, but I know when a man's smitten and when he's not, and I tell you Gilbert's smitten with Mildred. You mark my words—those two will get together one of these days. Then Mildred's going to be real disappointed. I've heard old Gilbert is as cold in the sack as yesterday's mashed potatoes."

Teal shook her head. As cold in the sack as yesterday's mashed potatoes? Poor Mildred.

"Well, I hope they do get together," Teal called back.

"Whatever for?"

"Because I think Mildred and Gilbert are lonely."

"What'd you say?" Ceil called from the bedroom.

"Nothing, Aunt Ceil." Teal let the subject drop. Ceil probably wouldn't agree anyway.

"You said something. I heard it."

"I was just talking to myself."

"Now that's a sure sign you're getting old. Is Fred Phillips going to buy the Electra?"

"Yes. He'll pick it up sometime Friday."

"Sure hate to see the thing go." A moment later Teal heard the door to Ceil's bedroom close.

When Teal went to bed herself, sleep didn't come easily. She lay in bed listening to the faint sounds of *The Arsenio Hall Show*, wondering what Bud was doing.

Had she made the right choice? Should she stay in Thirty-One Corners and seriously explore the possibility of marrying him? Her head was pounding and her heart was aching. So many questions, and she had no answers.

The mantel clock was chiming eight as Teal entered the kitchen the next morning. A brisk shower had cleared her head, and she was hoping that a cup of coffee would lift her spirits. Her flight was hours away, so she had ample time to pack and make last-minute arrangements for Ceil to enter Mortwiler's. Mason couldn't possibly marry

Ceil until he was fully recuperated, which could take a while.

The phone rang and Teal reached for it expectantly. Her heart plummeted when a woman's voice came over the wire.

"Teal?"

"Yes?"

"Hi! This is Amanda Hazelton. I just wanted to tell you how much I enjoyed the Auxiliary luncheon. It's not often we have someone with your talent to call upon."

"Thank you, Amanda. I appreciate your thoughtfulness."

"I was wondering . . . do you think you could squeeze some time in to cater a dinner for me next week? It's just a small gathering for a few of my husband's associates at the hospital—"

"I'm sorry, Amanda, I would love to, but I've booked a flight back to Washington this afternoon."

"Oh, really." Amanda sounded crushed. "You're leaving so soon?"

"I've already stayed longer than I originally planned. I'm afraid I can't neglect my business any longer."

"Oh . . . well, I was hoping you'd be here a while longer. I know of at least two other women who are planning to call you."

"I'm sorry." Teal fought the urge to slam the phone down and run. It was difficult enough to leave Bud without being reminded that her business could thrive in Thirty-One Corners.

After Amanda hung up, Teal had two more phone calls from women requesting that she cater their dinners.

Thoughtfully replacing the receiver after the

third call, she wondered if this was a devious plan to encourage her to stay. Each caller had been openly disappointed that she couldn't handle the event being planned, yet each had been polite and considerate. These women hadn't been hateful nor had they screamed at her like some of the Washington clients she'd had to refuse. Instead, the women of Thirty-One Corners had understood that her business needed her attention. And they had offered heartfelt condolences concerning Carl and Winnie before hanging up.

Instead of feeling guilty about turning away business, Teal had felt warmed by the genuine concern expressed by each caller. She had never realized how closely entwined people's lives were in small towns.

She moved to the window and surveyed the melon patch, her thoughts turning again to the question that she could not get out of her mind. *Could I be as content and as fulfilled if I moved back to Thirty-One Corners? Could I make a small-town doctor a suitable, loving, and nurturing wife?*

The questions both frightened and intrigued her. She couldn't imagine anyone nurturing Bud Huntington—with maybe one possible exception: herself.

"You're darn right I could make you a suitable wife, Bud Huntington," she whispered adamantly. "If I wanted to . . . and if you asked me. . . ."

"Asked you what?" Ceil said from behind her. "If you're going to talk to yourself, do it loud enough for me to hear."

"Sorry. I was just thinking."

"Well, I've got to get to church, then on to

Verda's. You're not leavin' for the airport until around two, are you?"

"No . . . not until two." Teal embraced the frail little woman affectionately. "I love you and I'm going to miss you, Aunt Ceil. I wish you'd come to Washington with me."

"I love you, too, even if you don't know a watermelon from a gnat's a—behind," Ceil corrected herself. After all, it was the Lord's day.

Teal grinned. "I think I might recognize the difference."

"Hmph." Ceil tilted her head to look Teal in the eye. "You might recognize a watermelon from a gnat's behind, but you don't know a thing about love. That's plain to see."

"Aunt Ceil." Teal's arms wearily dropped back to her sides. "I wish it was that simple."

"Well, don't throw the baby out with the bath water, that's all I've got to say."

Teal sighed patiently. "And what's that supposed to mean?"

"Bud might have been a hell-raiser when he was young, but you couldn't find a finer man if you looked forever. You'd be smart to go after him, Teal. Doc Huntington's got what it takes, and you'd be nuts to let him get away."

"Even if I were to admit that I'm in love with Bud—which I'm not—what makes you think he's in love with me?"

"Two things." Ceil folded her arms confidently. "I see the glow in his eye when he looks at you, and I happened to overhear the last part of your fight."

"Aunt Ceil! You eavesdropped on me?"

Ceil shrugged. "Even if I hadn't heard you two yelling at each other, a young man don't race out the drive like a bat out of hell in the middle of the night just because he was turned down for a date! I may be old, but I'm not simpleminded."

Sometimes Teal wished Ceil *wasn't* quite so sharp. "Well, we did have a little disagreement," Teal admitted.

"Disagreement?" Ceil shook her head wearily. "Plain old argument's more like it. I heard what you said and what he said, and *I* say you'd better come home and marry that boy before Sue Ellen Mosely does!"

A prickle of fear raced up Teal's spine as she recalled the pretty brunette Bud had been dancing with at the Legion hall. "Is Sue Ellen in love with Bud?"

"Every woman in town is in love with him!" she sputtered. "But don't worry." Ceil squeezed her shoulder sympathetically. "God made you for Bud Huntington. You're just too stubborn to see it."

"Aunt Ceil, Bud and I are so different." Teal began to pace the floor, wringing her hands.

"Nonsense. You'd be good for each other. All Bud needs is the love of a good woman to settle him down a bit, keep him from breaking his fool neck. And he'd be good for you. You're up there in Washington in a tiny little apartment, choking on those gas fumes, dodging all those cars, and putting up with all that crime and corruption. A person could flat croak living a life like that. And all you do is work. Winnie told me that. Just work, work, work. No time for lovin' kids or a husband. That's not normal. I'd be worrying about that if I were you."

Teal found herself fighting back tears. She wasn't sure what God intended for her. She wasn't sure of anything anymore.

"Of course, you're free to do anything you want,"

Ceil conceded. "But if it were me, I'd sure give some serious thought to what I've just been hearin'." Ceil plopped her hat on her head and jabbed it with a hat pin. "Winnie and Carl would have wanted me to set you straight on this, so don't go gettin' all bent out of shape once I'm gone. I'm only sayin' it for your own good."

"I'm not 'bent out of shape.' I just don't happen to agree with you."

"Well, too late to change things now, I guess. I got to be on my way or Mildred will be having a conniption fit." Ceil waved a lace handkerchief at Teal as she started toward the front door. She twisted the handle and turned to wink at Teal. "I'll tell you, if I wasn't so old, I'd have the hots for Bud myself."

Around noon Teal forced herself to eat a sandwich, even though it tasted like sawdust. Around two she carried her suitcases to the front door, then paused to take a final look around.

She was getting misty-eyed again when she heard a vehicle coming down the lane. She hurried to the window and saw Bud's pickup turning onto the drive.

When his knock sounded at the door, Teal hesitated. He knocked louder. Biting her lip, she reached to answer it.

Bud was standing there, his thumbs hooked into his belt, staring at her. He was dressed in the usual denim jeans and a broadcloth shirt open at the throat, yet somehow he didn't look as self-assured as he typically did.

"Hi."

"Hi." He glanced out across the melon patch,

apparently at a loss for words. In all the years Teal had known Bud Huntington, she had seen him in various forms, but never at a loss for words.

Teal didn't know what to say, either, so she just stood rigidly still, waiting for him to speak. She seriously doubted that he had come to apologize.

"When does your plane leave?"

"Four. I was just on my way out." She motioned lamely toward her suitcases in the hallway.

"Look, I've got a private plane at the airport in Sikeston. I'd like to fly you back to Washington if you'd let me."

"That isn't necessary. . . ."

"I don't mind."

Though her heart leapt at the chance to spend more time with him, Teal realized that it would only protract the pain. If a relationship between them was impossible, then she wanted a clean break now.

"I don't think that would be wise," she refused softly.

Something very close to anger flashed in his eyes, but he managed to suppress it. "I'm just offering you a ride, not a lifetime commitment. I need to do this, Teal. Allow me this one concession."

Of course he would never apologize. That wasn't Bud Huntington's way. Women flocked to him, didn't they? All he had to do was choose one of many who scrambled after him. Why would he be interested in a snooty priss who didn't want to live in a town where everyone knew her and where gumbo stuck to her shoes? Against her better judgment, she muttered, "All right."

The plane turned out to be a silver and blue two-seater. Teal waited while Bud filed the flight plan, then accepted his assistance to climb aboard. She watched, fascinated, as he checked his instruments and waited for clearance. If she'd had any doubt about his being a capable pilot, his thoroughness convinced her otherwise. She caught herself wondering what other surprises he was hiding. It seemed that sometime in the past twelve years he'd developed several interesting facets that she never would have dreamed possible.

The takeoff was perfect. As they soared into a clear blue sky Teal wondered if she had lost her mind—yet she knew she hadn't. If she could spend one more day with him, painful as it might be, she would.

Staring out the cockpit window, she was fascinated by the view of the earth from a low altitude, a view that she'd never had from a larger plane. The ground looked like a crazy patchwork quilt— different shades of green and gold and brown. The blue of a river threaded through the fields, and dots of houses decorated the landscape. The mighty Mississippi and the Ohio merged in a brown roil beneath her as tugboats worked their way down the river hauling tons of grain and other cargo.

Seeing it all from this angle was a little like seeing Bud again when she'd first come home. Without giving it much thought, she had expected him to remain exactly as she'd left him. Just as she'd expected everything in Thirty-One Corners to be exactly as she'd left it. But from this perspective the town took on a whole new dimension, and so did the man.

"I guess that's what's so confusing," Teal murmured.

"What?"

She was startled to realize that she'd spoken. "Nothing. I was just thinking aloud."

His dark gaze surveyed the dark circles beneath her eyes. "We'll have to refuel later. We'll eat then."

"Okay," she murmured.

They landed at a small airport and ate at a sandwich shop inside a tiny terminal, saying little. They reboarded the plane in silence.

If he doesn't want to talk to me, why is he flying me back to Washington? she agonized.

The rest of the flight was just as uneventful and just as silent.

As the plane touched down on a small private strip outside Washington, Teal was uncertain what to say. A brisk thank-you seemed inadequate. There was too much left unfinished between them.

"I'll call a cab," Teal said as they entered the terminal.

"I've already taken care of that."

When the cab arrived, Bud slipped her suitcases and his overnight bag into the trunk while Teal gave the driver the address of her apartment.

The ride into the city was as strained as the flight. Teal caught the driver curiously glancing at the silent couple as they sat with as much space between them as possible, each looking out separate windows in silence.

When they arrived at her apartment building, Teal got out and started to pay the driver, but Bud stopped her.

"I'll take care of it. I'll be going on to a hotel."

Leaving instructions with the driver to wait, Bud gathered her luggage and walked into the building with her.

Teal's apartment was on the first floor. She

found her hands trembling as she inserted the key into the lock. She felt his presence so acutely that it was a torment. She unlocked the door, stepped inside, and snapped on a light.

The apartment felt stuffy and abandoned, as if she'd been gone months instead of weeks.

"I'll open a window," she murmured.

Bud set the suitcases inside the doorway and glanced around her apartment. It had a homey feel that he hadn't anticipated. He'd expected chrome and glass. Instead, it looked more relaxed, less formal. There were lush ferns in front of a wide window, and framed photographs on a table that served as a desk. He recognized several shots of Carl and Winnie and Ceil, along with pictures of Teal.

Bud crossed the room to study the photos while she walked through her apartment switching on lights.

There were photos of Teal as a child and at ages ten and fifteen. A graduation picture of her standing arm and arm with Winnie and Carl held a prominent position in the center of the table. Apparently, she hadn't left everything behind when she'd left Thirty-One Corners.

"I don't remember this," he said, picking up a class photo of kids lined up in front of their high school.

"It was in the yearbook. You probably wouldn't remember it. It was my home economics class."

"Oh, yes. There's Mary Lou Waterman." He set the picture down and smiled a little.

Teal sighed. "Lately, there have been times when I wish we could go back to those days. . . ." Her voice broke, and she looked away quickly.

"And I was hoping we could get on with our

lives." Turning back to the pictures, he picked up the one of her home economics class again. "If I remember right, you couldn't boil water."

Teal had to smile. "I was trying to learn how to boil water. I got pretty good at it by the time I graduated."

He glanced up, and their eyes met. A moment later they exchanged forgiving smiles.

"Well, guess I'd better go," he began, remembering that the meter on the cab was still running.

"Where will you stay?"

"I don't know. I'll find something?"

"Stay with me," she said impulsively. She couldn't believe that she'd said it, but then it dawned on her that the thought had been in the back of her mind all day. She couldn't let him go like that. She loved him too much.

He gazed at her, his features growing solemn. "Is that what you want?"

"It's late. There's no sense in you looking for a hotel at this hour. Stay, and I promise you fresh apple pancakes in the morning."

"If I stay, I'll want more than apple pancakes," he said quietly.

"I know," she whispered. "So will I."

"What should I do about the cab?"

"It will go away eventually."

"We owe the fare."

"Then it will come back eventually."

Taking her hand, he drew her to him. Teal moved into his arms, painfully aware of her need for him. She wanted him as badly as the hunger in his eyes revealed that he wanted her.

And when she awoke the next morning and found him gone, she realized that it was the only way either of them could have said good-bye.

Ten

"Tell Mrs. Lowther that if she wants lilacs this time of year, it's going to cost her an arm and a leg."

"I told her, but she said it was her understanding that lilacs were included in the price you quoted."

"Then she misunderstood."

"I realize that, but what do I tell her?"

Teal knew what she'd like for Phyllis to tell her. She slid the bottom drawer of her desk open and fumbled for a bottle of aspirin. "I don't know, Phyllis. I'll see what I can do and get back to you."

For the past week, Teal had thrown herself into her business, finishing details on projects that were already begun and trying to woo new clients. She was like a demon, working from early morning to late at night—and she'd never felt more unhappy.

In a moment of weakness she'd found herself picking up the phone and dialing information for the number of the hospital in Thirty-One Corners. She'd told herself she was only calling Bud to find

out how Mason was doing. Ceil had written to say that Mason had been released from the hospital but that Bud was still keeping a close eye on him.

Because Bud had been in surgery that day, she had hung up without leaving a message. She wondered what would she have said? *I'm lonely. I'm more confused than ever. I miss you. I want you. I adore you. . . . I love you.*

Leaning back in her chair, Teal stared at the phone. Would he be in surgery that morning?

She bit her lower lip and leaned forward in her chair, reaching for the receiver cautiously. She was being a fool. If he still felt as deeply about her as she felt about him, he would have called by now. *A week* had gone by since she'd left Thirty-One Corners, and he hadn't called once.

A voice she didn't recognize announced, "Sheney Hospital."

"Dr. Huntington, please."

"Is this an emergency?"

"No." *Only if an aching heart is an emergency.*

"May I say who's calling?"

She swallowed and was astonished to hear the vulnerability in her voice when she answered, "Teal Anderson."

"Thank you. One moment, please."

Teal waited, her fingers gripping the receiver. What if he wouldn't talk to her? What if—

"Teal?" Bud took the line immediately.

"Hi. Hope I'm not catching you at a bad time."

"Not at all. How's Washington?"

"Fine, just fine."

An awkward silence fell between them as Teal searched for an excuse for her call.

"I had a letter from Aunt Ceil yesterday," she finally said.

"That's good. She's doing fine. I stopped by to see her last week."

"She said the flowers you brought her were lovely. Thank you. That was nice of you."

"My pleasure. I'm glad she enjoyed them."

Teal paused to draw a breath. "She said Mason was doing very well, but I just, uh, I thought I'd call and see what you thought."

"Mason's doing well. Actually, he's recuperating faster than I thought he would. By the way, it looks like you're going to be invited to a wedding before too many more weeks."

Her heart leapt. "A wedding?"

"Mason tells me that he and Ceil have been talking about getting married."

Teal smiled. "Ceil's been working on getting Mason to propose to her for years."

"Well, it looks like she's finally worn him down."

"Worn him down?"

"Sorry," he said lightly. "She's helped him see the light. Think it can work out?"

"Sure. Why not?"

"Sure. Why not. How are things going with you?"

"Oh, fine. Busy. And you?"

"The same—I'm sorry, Teal, I'm being paged."

"That's okay. Take care."

"You too."

Bud replaced the receiver slowly, then leaned back in his chair to stare at the ceiling. He hadn't been paged. He'd just found it hard to talk to her. Hearing her voice had brought back vivid memories of the few weeks they had shared. Not that those memories were ever far from his mind. In the past few days he had picked up the phone more than once to call and beg her to come home.

Yet each time, common sense had stopped him. If Teal were to return, it would have to be because she wanted to, not because he had pressured her into it.

The second time Teal phoned Bud was almost exactly a week later. She noticed that her fingers were trembling as she dialed the number. After she asked for Bud, she started to hang up, but then his voice came over the line.

"Dr. Huntington."

"Bud? Hi," she began, trying to sound cheery. "I hope this isn't a bad time?"

"No, I just finished rounds. How are you doing?"

"Tired. I can't seem to get into the swing of things again." She laughed. "It's like walking in gumbo—each step gets a little heavier."

"You need to find a good man, settle down, and not work so hard."

"Yeah." She smiled. "I've thought of that."

"I saw Harvey yesterday. He said the melon harvest is finished and the bank has an offer on the farm."

"That's what I understand."

"Who bought it?"

"I'm not sure. Mr. Greer didn't say."

"I'm sure you're relieved to get it sold."

"Well, yes . . . I'm happy. Like you once said, it could be a nice place. Those tall trees, that wonderful wide porch. Of course, whoever buys it will have some repairs to do. I noticed the roof was beginning to leak."

"The roof leaks?"

"Not a lot, but some," she admitted.

She heard him mutter an oath under his breath.

"What?"

"Nothing. I just spilled my coffee."

"Oh." Silence prevailed as she tried to think of something else to say. When she failed to come up with anything plausible, she finally murmured, "Well, I'm sure you're busy."

"Not that busy." He paused, then admitted softly, "I miss you, Teal. I went fishing the other day and got caught in a shower, and I thought of you."

Leaning back in her chair, she felt herself growing weak with longing for him. "I miss you too."

"I guess I should apologize for the way I slipped away that night I took you back to Washington."

"No need to apologize. When I awoke and found that you'd gone, I guess a part of me felt relieved. I'm . . . not very good at saying good-bye."

There was another heavy silence before his voice came over the wire. "I love you, Teal."

Tears stung her eyes. "You don't have to say that, you know."

"No, but it's important to me that you know."

The fourth week crawled by. Teal tried to fill each minute with work to keep from thinking, but the hours and the minutes were relentless. Somehow the satisfaction she'd felt from her work—the work she'd once gloried in—was gone. All the tiny details that she'd once taken such great pride in taking care of seemed tedious and exhausting. Even Phyllis noticed her distraction and irritability.

"What *is* the matter with you?" Phyllis finally asked at the end of the week.

"Matter with me? Nothing. Why?"

"You're here, but you're not here. Having trouble with your aunt and uncle's estate?"

"No." Teal pushed away from her desk. She

turned her back and strode to the file cabinet. "Everything's fine. In fact, the farm has been sold. It's possible that I'll be going back to Thirty-One Corners any day now to sign the papers." She glanced outside and was surprised to see that it was already dark. "What time it it?"

"Nine."

"Nine?"

"Nine," Phyllis repeated patiently. "As in, nine o'clock at night, on a Friday, when most single, attractive women have dates."

"Oh." Teal absently reached for a folder, then shut the file drawer. "I'm sorry. I have been demanding a lot of your time lately."

Phyllis sank onto a chair in front of Teal's desk. "I may be out of place, but I'm worried about you. You act like a woman who's running from someone or something."

Teal paused at the large window overlooking the lighted Washington landscape. "Am I that transparent?"

"It was tough going home, wasn't it?"

"More than I expected it to be."

"Saying good-bye is never easy," Phyllis ventured.

"Neither is saying hello again."

"Hello?"

Teal smiled vaguely as she moved back to her desk. "I met a guy I'd gone to high school with."

"Sounds interesting. Tell me more."

"He's a doctor now."

"Good-looking?"

"Kevin Costner, Mel Gibson, and Scott Bakula rolled into one."

"Check it out!"

"And he's just as devil-may-care as ever. Thirty-

One Corners's version of James Dean. He specialized in dating the wildest girls he could find."

"Let me guess." Phyllis held up her hand. "Now
he's changed. Now he's a fine, upstanding citizen
of the community."

"Well, I suppose he is," Teal said, "but he still
rides motorcycles and bucking broncos and drives
race cars. He's also a good doctor, well-loved and
respected in Thirty-One Corners."

"Sounds like a dream come true. A doctor who
looks like Kevin Costner, Mel Gibson, and Scott
Bakula rolled into one. And this is a problem?"

"Just one," Teal admitted.

"What? You want to pick up where you left off
years ago, but he's engaged to this gorgeous blond
with a rich father?"

Teal laughed lightly. "Not exactly. Bud and I were
like oil and water in high school, and he's not
engaged to anyone."

"So, *what's* the problem?"

"I *love* him. That's the problem."

"That's great!" She exclaimed.

"No, it isn't!"

"Why not?"

"Who was it who said you can never go home
again?" Teal drew a deep breath. "I guess whoever
it was just wasn't tired enough."

"Tired or bored?"

"You're too perceptive," Teal accused. "Okay, so I
guess the glitz is gone, the gilt is peeling off the
rose, the bright lights have dimmed. Whatever.
Maybe I am just tired, or maybe my values have
changed. I don't know, Phyllis. I honestly think
that I'm in love with the man, and I don't know
what to do about it."

"Seriously? You don't think it was just the nostalgia of going home again combined with the fact that you're particularly vulnerable right now?

"It's more than that," Teal said thoughtfully, gazing out the window again. "I find myself thinking about Saturday night dances at the Legion hall, and Fourth of July picnics at the park, and playing bingo on Wednesday nights. It's crazy. The very things I left Thirty-One Corners to get away from are the very things that seem to be drawing me back."

"Maybe it's just the sentimental journey—"

"No, it's The Greek."

"The Greek?" Phyllis repeated. "Who's The Greek?"

"Burgess 'Bud' Huntington, nicknamed The Greek because he looked like a Greek god."

"Uh-oh," Phyllis teased. "Sounds to me like you have a serious problem. "I've never seen you act this way, even about Senator York."

"I wasn't in love with David. I realize that now more than ever."

Teal swung around and stared at her assistant. "Phyllis, I'm seriously thinking about returning to Thirty-One Corners and asking Bud Huntington to marry me."

"You're serious about this, aren't you?"

"Yes."

"Then go for it."

"We have two very different personalities. I'm terrified it won't work out."

"If you were alike, it would be boring."

"But I thought I hated living in Thirty-One Corners."

"So, you left for a while, got all the resentment out of your system, and found out that life isn't always greener on the other side of the fence. Now you can go to Thirty-One Corners, marry your doctor, and tell your grandchildren about how you moved to the big city, became a successful businesswoman, and found that in the end all that really matters is where your heart is." Phyllis's features softened. "You know, Teal, not many people have the chance to find real happiness. If you honestly think you've got a shot at it with Bud, go for it. The two of you might have to work a little at dissolving your differences, but if you love each other, it won't be a sacrifice, just pure pleasure when it all comes together."

Teal gazed back at her friend, amazed at how simple the answer was.

"Just like that?"

Phyllis shrugged. "Just like that. Besides, what's the benefit of being a woman if you don't exercise your prerogative to change your mind?"

"What about the business?"

"Make me the right deal, and you've just sold it."

"I'd want to keep the name Teal's Tidbits. I'm not dying, just getting married. I'll want to open a catering business again once I've had a few months alone with my husband."

"Agreed."

"And you have to promise to come to Thirty-One Corners to see me once a year."

"Any more men down there like this doctor of yours?"

Teal smiled. "No, and this doctor is all mine, Phyllis. All mine."

"That's what I was afraid of, but if they ever clone him, let me know, will you, hon?"

"Oh, Phyllis." Teal stood up, trembling like a child. "Do I dare follow my heart?"

Phyllis smiled. "I think the question is do you dare not?"

It was early evening when Teal carried her overnight bag into the empty farmhouse. The scent of honeysuckle was faint now, but the smell of home was strong in the air.

Her first stop after arriving in Thirty-One Corners had been at the bank to sign the sale contract on Carl and Winnie's farm. She hadn't been surprised to learn from Wallace Greer that Bud was the purchaser. She'd realized that he had just given her the best gift she had ever had.

Wallace was nice enough to drive her to the house. "Doc said he's always had a fondness for this old place. Says he plans to restore the house, give it a touch of paint and a new roof," he commented as he opened a window to let in some fresh air. "Should look real nice when he's finished. Winnie and Carl would be real pleased. Bud wasn't sure how you'd feel about it though."

"I think it's wonderful," Teal said as she happily wandered around the empty rooms, letting her imagination fill them with new furniture. A comfortable sofa and love seat flanking the fireplace and a large, leather chair for Bud. Oak tables and an antique secretary in front of the window. "In fact, it's just perfect."

"Don't know what Doc plans to do with a house this large, him being single and all. Maybe he'll marry that Sue Ellen Mosely one of these days."

Teal grinned. "Maybe, maybe not, but I'm sure he'll make good use of the place."

Wallace dusted his hands lightly. "As soon as you

get those few things from the attic you want, you'll lock up for me, won't you?"

"I certainly will. Thanks, Mr. Greer. You've been a wonderful help."

"Just leave the key under the mat. I'll tell Bud where it is."

"I will."

The moment Wallace's car pulled out of the drive Teal raced back to her rental car.

Within twenty minutes she was pulling into the parking lot at the hospital. Her pulse raced and her stomach felt slightly queasy when she saw Bud's pickup parked in his reserved space. She hadn't been sure that Bud was working tonight, but she figured a higher power was looking over her, so he just had to be.

The antiseptic hospital smell made her wrinkle her nose as she hurried to the elevator. *Please, don't let him be in surgery*. She paced back and forth and punched the button a second time. *What can I tell him? I've changed my mind? I've grown up? Let's get married tonight. Kiss me or I'm going to die? All of the above? None of the above?*

She stepped off the elevator onto the second floor and hurried down the corridor toward his office, chanting softly, "Let him be here, let him be here."

She opened the door to his office, and her heart sank when she saw that it was empty. A small lamp was burning on the cluttered desk, illuminating the stethoscope lying beside a half cup of cold coffee.

Closing the door, she turned and hurried back down the hallway toward the emergency room.

She took the stairs because it seemed faster. Racing down the first-floor corridor, she suddenly collided with a pink-coated volunteer, nearly knocking the woman off her feet.

As Teal paused to steady the woman and the bouquet of flowers that she was carrying, she recognized Amanda Hazelton, and her face broke into a smile.

"Teal?" Amanda asked, stunned.

"Can't talk now, Amanda," Teal apologized hurriedly, "but give me a call sometime next week. I'm moving Teal's Tidbits to Thirty-One Corners, and I would love to have your business."

"What . . . why are you . . . I thought you were . . ." Amanda sputtered.

"I'm back," Teal called as she raced on down the corridor.

"For good?"

"For *good*." Teal disappeared around the corner, leaving Amanda to stare after her blankly.

She turned the next corner and went weak with relief as she spotted Bud and two other doctors striding down the corridor ahead of her. Dear Lord, what if he didn't want to marry her? The thought had not entered her mind until then. Well, she would make him want to marry her.

"Bud!"

Turning, Bud saw Teal running toward him. For a moment he wasn't sure he was seeing correctly, then he called, "Teal?"

She was breathless when she finally caught up with him. "Hello, Dr. Sheney, Dr. Miller."

The two older doctors nodded their greeting.

Her eyes turned to Bud, and her heart caught in her throat at the sight of his familiar handsome features. Oh, how she had missed him! "Have I caught you at a bad time?"

"I'm . . . on my way to surgery—"

"Then I won't delay you. Mind if I walk along with you?" Catching Bud's hand, she fell into step beside the three men.

"Teal, what are you doing here?" Bud whispered. "I've tried to call you for days!"

"Don't talk, just listen. I've changed my 'stubborn' mind. Will you marry me?"

Bud's eyes met hers as he attempted to keep pace with the two other doctors. "Yes."

"Good, because I would hate to have to beg."

"Teal . . ." Closing his eyes, Bud caught her to him. "Are you sure?"

"Very, very sure."

His mouth lowered to take hers in a masterfully possessive kiss.

Aware that the two other doctors were gawking at them, she pulled back and gazed up at him. "I love you so much. I'm sorry it's taken me so long to realize it."

"Time doesn't matter, as long as you do realize it. And you will marry me," he added for fear she might back out.

"I'll marry you whenever you say."

"One week from today."

"A week?" She thought about it for a moment, then smiled. "One from today, Dr. Huntington. But you'll have to put me up at your place since I've sold the farm."

He lowered his mouth to meet hers again. "I think I can live with that."

Dr. Sheney and Dr. Miller exchanged amused glances as the small entourage drew closer to the operating room.

"Look, I won't promise to have your meal on the table every night at five sharp because I'll have my own business to run—"

"Good, because I won't be there every evening at five sharp," Bud promised.

"A husband with a wife who has a catering business shouldn't expect his home to be run on a regular schedule," she warned.

"The same goes for the wife of a doctor."

"And I'll want to travel some. It will be rather nice living in a small town again, but I'll still want to go to Paris and Holland and Germany and the Orient—"

"I was thinking maybe Hawaii for the honeymoon, then Paris in the spring. Okay with you?"

"Okay with me."

Their mouths drifted together again, and their footsteps slowed long enough for them to hold on to each other tightly.

"I've missed you," he whispered huskily in her ear. "What took you so long to change your mind?"

"I guess I am stubborn. Can you live with that one small imperfection?"

"Ah, Teal, my love. You're close to perfect in my eyes."

She frowned. "Only close?"

"Close enough to make me a happy man."

"Well, I'll try to be understanding about your bronc riding and stock car racing and early-morning fishing and whatever other crazy thing you get it into your head to do," she said as they hurried to catch up with the two doctors.

He flashed her that boyish grin, and she knew she wasn't fooling him. She would let him do anything he wanted. "You know, I can change, too," he said. "Or at least meet you halfway on subjects we don't agree on."

"And when the children come—"

His look grew tender. "When the children come,

I'll be too busy being a father to pursue other hobbies."

"And about this earthquake thing, Bud. Personally, I don't put much credence in the prediction. I don't really believe there's going to *be* an earthquake, but as a precaution, maybe we should think about getting a whistle."

"Why not? It'll give Ceil something to do."

Squeezing him tightly about the waist, she gave him a suggestive wink. "Just one more thing."

"You got it."

"You have to promise that you'll show me just how much you missed me when we're alone later," she whispered.

"Not only later, but I plan on showing you for the rest of my life."

They paused in front of the operating room doors, their mouths meeting in another long, searing kiss, and this time the floor did move. Lifting their heads, they saw puzzlement in each other's eyes.

"Did you feel that?"

"Yes. Was it the quake?"

"I'm not sure. . . ."

They looked around the corridors for signs of disruption, but the nurses were casually going about their work.

Dr. Sheney and Dr. Miller paused in the open doorway.

"Dr. Huntington, Mrs. Gilbert's bypass?" Dr. Sheney reminded pleasantly.

"Be right there. Did you feel anything a minute ago?"

The two older doctors exchanged another amused glance. "Not a thing, Bud. It must be love."

Teal smiled. *It must be love.* Her face was glowing as Bud kissed her one final time before he reluctantly disappeared into the operating room.

Whirling, she walked on air to the waiting room, bubbling over with happiness.

Teal Anderson was going to marry the wildest boy in town, and she couldn't wait.

Epilogue

December 3, 1990, the day of Iben Browning's predicted earthquake, the day citizens of Thirty-One Corners—and the nation—had awaited for months . . .

Wallace Greer washed his car.

Amanda Hazelton went Christmas shopping, though the media satellite trucks flooding the town backed up traffic for miles.

The Mettersons' dog ran away again, and it took the neighbors all day to find it.

Ceil Anderson had Nettie Baker's son drive her and Nettie to town so they could buy novelty T-shirts. Nettie's read "It's Our Fault" and Ceil's said "Visit Thirty-One Corners (While It's Still Here)." The shirts were priced at $10.00 for adults and $7.50 for children. Ceil didn't think the prices were bad, but Nettie declared them highway robbery.

Mildred Yarnell had her hair and nails done, just in case. That evening she ventured out to join her husband for an "Aftershock" drink at the Elk's Lodge.

Joleen Ferguson took her baby to the pediatrician for a checkup, then stopped at Wilson's Café for a "Quake Burger" and fries before tackling her weekly shopping at Piggly Wiggly.

Mason stayed home and rested because Doc Huntington didn't want him getting excited before his honeymoon.

Teal and Bud went shopping for baby clothes.

The earthquake that everyone had prepared for and dreaded failed to occur.

Iben Browning could not be reached for comment.

THE EDITOR'S CORNER

With the six marvelous **LOVESWEPT**s coming your way next month, it certainly will be the season to be jolly. Reading the best romances from the finest authors—what better way to enter into the holiday spirit?

Leading our fabulous lineup is the ever-popular Fayrene Preston with **SATAN'S ANGEL**, LOVESWEPT #510. Nicholas Santini awakes after a car crash and thinks he's died and gone to heaven—why else would a beautiful angel be at his side? But Angel Smith is a flesh-and-blood woman who makes him burn with a desire that lets him know he's very much alive. Angel's determined to work a miracle on this magnificent man, to drive away the pain—and the peril—that torments him. A truly wonderful story, written with sizzling sensuality and poignant emotions—one of Fayrene's best!

How appropriate that Gail Douglas's newest LOVESWEPT is titled **AFTER HOURS**, #511, for that's when things heat up between Casey McIntyre and Alex McLean. Alex puts his business—and heart—on the line when he works *very* closely with Casey to save his newspaper. He's been betrayed before, but Casey inspires trust . . . and brings him to a fever pitch of sensual excitement. She never takes orders from anyone, yet she can't seem to deny Alex's passionate demands. A terrific book, from start to finish.

Sandra Chastain weaves her magical touch in **THE-JUDGE AND THE GYPSY**, LOVESWEPT #512. When Judge Rasch Webber unknowingly shatters her father's dream, Savannah Ramey vows a Gypsy's revenge: She would tantalize him beyond reason, awakening longings he's denied, then steal what he most loves. She couldn't know she'd be entangled in a web of desire, drawn to the velvet caress of Rasch's voice and the ecstatic fulfillment in his arms. You'll be thoroughly enchanted with this story of forbidden love.

The combination of love and laughter makes **MIDNIGHT KISS** by Marcia Evanick, LOVESWEPT #513, completely irresistible. To Autumn O'Neil, Thane Clayborne is a sexy stick-in-the-mud, and she delights in making him lose control. True, running a little wild is not Thane's style, but Autumn's seductive beauty tempts him to let go. Still, she's afraid that the man who bravely sacrificed a dream for another's happiness could never care for a woman who ran scared when it counted most. Another winner from Marcia Evanick!

With his tight jeans, biker boots, and heartbreak-blue eyes, Michael Hayward is a **TEMPTATION FROM THE PAST,** LOVESWEPT #514, by Cindy Gerard. January Stewart has never seen a sexier man, but she knows he's more trouble that she can handle. Intrigued by the dedicated lawyer, Michael wants to thaw January's cool demeanor and light her fire. Is he the one who would break down her defenses and cast away her secret pain? Your heart will be stirred by this touching story.

A fitting final course is **JUST DESSERTS** by Theresa Gladden, LOVESWEPT #515. Caitlin MacKenzie has had it with being teased by her new housemate, Drew Daniels, and she retaliates with a cream pie in his face! Pleased that serious Caitie has a sense of humor to match her lovely self, Drew begins an ardent pursuit. She would fit so perfectly in the future he's mapped out, but Catie has dreams of her own, dreams that could cost her what she has grown to treasure. A sweet and sexy romance—what more could anybody want?

FANFARE presents four truly spectacular books this month! Don't miss bestselling Amanda Quick's **RENDEZVOUS.** From London's most exclusive club to an imposing country manor, comes this provocative tale about a free-thinking beauty, a reckless charmer, and a love that defied all logic. **MIRACLE,** by beloved LOVESWEPT author Deborah Smith, is the unforgettable contemporary romance of passion and the collision of worlds, where a man and a woman who couldn't have been more different learn that love may be improbable, but never impossible.

Immensely talented Rosalind Laker delivers the exquisite historical **CIRCLE OF PEARLS.** In England during the days of plague and fire, Julia Pallister's greatest test comes from an unexpected quarter—the man she calls enemy, a man who will stop at nothing to win her heart. And in **FOREVER,** by critically acclaimed Theresa Weir, we witness the true power of love. Sammy Thoreau had been pronounced a lost cause, but from the moment Dr. Rachel Collins lays eyes on him, she knows she would do anything to help the bad-boy journalist learn to live again.

Happy reading!

With every good wish for a holiday filled with the best things in life,

Nita Taublib

Nita Taublib
Associate Publisher/LOVESWEPT
Publishing Associate/FANFARE

"Funny and heartrending . . . wonderful characters . . . I laughed out loud and couldn't stop reading. A splendid romance!" -- *Susan Elizabeth Phillips*, <u>New York Times</u> *bestselling author of FANCY PANTS and HOT SHOT*

Miracle

by

Deborah Smith

An unforgettable story of love and the collision of two worlds. From a shanty in the Georgia hills to a television studio in L.A., from the heat and dust of Africa to glittering Paris nights -- with warm, humorous, passionate characters, MIRACLE weaves a spell in which love may be improbable but never impossible.